Charles F. Hotchkiss

On the Ebb

A Few Log-Lines from an Old Salt

Charles F. Hotchkiss

On the Ebb
A Few Log-Lines from an Old Salt

ISBN/EAN: 9783337058111

Printed in Europe, USA, Canada, Australia, Japan

Cover: Foto ©Andreas Hilbeck / pixelio.de

More available books at **www.hansebooks.com**

ON THE EBB:

A FEW

Log-Lines from an Old Salt

CHARLES F. HOTCHKISS.

NEW HAVEN:

TUTTLE, MOREHOUSE & TAYLOR, PRINTERS.

1878.

PREFACE.

I PROPOSE to launch this little book out into the great maelstrom of this busy world, not doubting that I shall live as long and equally as happy as if the event had never occurred. It is in plain style, exactly as is my way of conversation. There never was much fog about me, except when fishing off Cuttyhunk or Nantucket Shoals; and I never fished there without being enveloped in it. The cure for that is a pocket compass, a good dry boat, a lead line and plenty of bait. I never called a "Blue-fish" by a wrong name, nor the "Porgie" a "Scup." The "Sea Bass" is not a "Hannah Hill," nor is the "Weak Fish" a "Salt Water Trout." I could not use great high-toned words in these pages even if I wished to; nor do I believe that my readers will be of that class who swallow great swelling words of man's wisdom and invention. I have no excuse to offer the public for any absence of punctuation or grammar, for the printer, like the underwriter, is responsible for those useful arrangements.

It is my business, and mine alone, to work up some of the incidents of 73 years, put it in pamphlet form, pay the printer and sell it, provided it has merit. It stands on its own bottom. If the purchaser, after getting possession, has made a satisfactory bargain, we are even; and if he, she or it, is not suited, we are even again. It was my barrel of flour, or my string of fish, and as I never recommended the quality, they should have looked the horse in the mouth. I do not send the fish to market in a wheel-barrow, trumpeting the quality or kind—it is your business to open its gills; for who would cry "Stale fish?" I am too old to meddle with fiction in any shape, for it is much easier to catch fish with good, clean, live bait, than an old dead winkle. Fish are not fools always, neither are the majority of the human family full of wisdom. My experience, piscatorially, (as my friends will endorse,) has been *large*, *long* and *deep*, and at my stand-point of life, I have concluded that *game fish* are much more smart than the human family, for they never take stinking bait in their mouth, consequently they never vomit. No, never! Mankind swoops up everything of the book species that is announced, provided it comes under Turkey Morocco and Gold Leaf. I send this book out in its plain Quaker garb, extracting from it all the *scales*, *flippers*, *backbone*, *head* and *inwards*, leaving the purchaser the clear marrow. In fact, it is like a Connecticut River Shad, all washed clean of fiction, "well *bloated*," and ready for broiling. It was not indeed necessary to pay well-known literary men $100 to do this work of cleaning my fish for market. I have a good wife at home, and between us both we succeed, as I think, successfully; at any rate, we are equally interested in the welfare or success of the thing, and our services are free; this all helps the purchaser—and we have decided that the Fish is worth One Dollar. Reader, what do you think?

But before I close my Preface, let me say, seriously, you will find in the book the narrative of a voyage occupying six months in the brig Shepherdess, Captain Peter Storer, Master, with whom the author made several voyages in early life, commencing as cabin boy. It is rather lengthy, but as a matter of history I think you will find it interesting. The good old captain is well known as a perfect sailor and a strict disciplinarian. He is alive now—as good as new, and eighty-seven years old at that. He was my schoolmaster when I was suffering with that dreadful complaint, the "13-year-old fever," yet instructed me outside the usual "Iron Rule" enforced by the "rope's end," in which discipline many a boy has been ruined. His word was law, and different from many other skippers, he knew when men did their duty. My education under him has endeared him to me, and I take great pleasure in respectfully dedicating that portion of the little book to him, and add the following, as breathing the true sentiments of my soul:

> " Let day improve on day, and year on year,
> Without a pain, a trouble or a fear,
> Till death unfelt that tender frame destroy
> In some soft dream, or ecstacy of joy;
> Peaceful sleep out the Sabbath of the tomb,
> And wake to raptures in a life to come."

You will also find my Trip to California in 1849, with many interesting incidents. The voyage with Captain Peter Storer, alluded to before, is full of incident—nautical, historical, piscatorial and spice; but it is truth. Sam Patch's last leap at Genesee Falls, showing, as Sam said, "some things can be done as well as others;" and I think the Dish of Chowder of the author, with his "Rolling Stone gathers no Moss;" the Fish, Fishing and Fishing Places, to choose, will at least give a good revenue for the book, if it does not immortalize his name.

C. F. HOTCHKISS.

Short Beach, Branford, Conn., April, 1878.

CONTENTS.

A DISH OF CHOWDER.

A little on the subject of "A Rolling Stone gathers no Moss."—Something on Old Age.—Considerable on Fish, Fishermen and Fishing places.—A small sprinkling on "Respect due old Fishermen," and Anathemas on those who disturb others in fishing.

"A ROLLING STONE GATHERS NO MOSS."

THE author is now too old to gain much wisdom from this spicy saying. His opportunities are much like a shoal of blue fish—all gone by. The tide of life has made its ebb and the fish are all outside the bar, where it needs nerve and a strong arm to stem the tide with the oars and make a good cast of the squid in the surf. I cheerfully accept the circumstances and must be content with shore fishing, where things are quiet and the fish smaller. The future of my fishing must be in smoother waters, a small skiff, nicely moored in the eddy of the tide, keeping a good lookout for squalls, and always a harbor under my lee, choice basket of snack, a small bottle of good Grenada (20 years old), a neat little locker in the stern sheets, plenty of good fresh bait and jack-knife; compass in my pocket, a good clear sun overhead, and a plenty of time to stay the tide out and in, —not encumbered with a greenhorn cousin hailing from the Green Mountains, stepping around the boat as if a "fiddler" had him by the big toe, or flirting fish hooks loosely in the air, apparently trying to see how near he can come to my old gray eyes and not hit; or yelling sufficiently loud to frighten every fish off the reef in telling me how he kept school, and how he used to fish for dace with pin hooks, and then how he fell in love with Mary. No, no! I have made all the noise in the world that I propose to make (unless I set the world on fire by this book), and as I prefer a "still hunt" so do I prefer to get into my dingey alone. Yes, quietly, alone! unless, perhaps, a lady at the breakfast table begs a chance with me for the voyage, conditional that her dear little five-year old Judy shall remain at home, and that short skirts shall be the order for the day, because an eight-foot boat can't hold everything. Long trails are much better operating on a sidewalk than as a bailing dish to a boat. When the ladies, dear souls! get into my boat with these trails, I admire them so much for soaking up the water, that I quietly put my two large sponges in the locker. Then every tub is on its own bottom.

But the matter of Fishing. Why so much of it? Can it be possible that you adopt it as the best hobby you can ride? Yes; I certainly have. I favor it first from inclination, for I was born under the zodiac sign, the "feet." It is a healthy and amusing hobby. It can be enjoyed with more economy, and the fish as a food feeds the brain; and beside, while enjoying this hobby, the mind is improved. It is a glorious good place for reflection, and with a good Havana cigar it tends to make a person forget his enemies and forgive his friends. He is even more charitable to the poor; his surplus game goes Scott free to his friends, the rich and poor alike. It is not like the Fast Horse hobby (your 2.20 horse), for which you have just paid $5,000 more or less, and who died last night. Perhaps his death saved your life, the day after! With a horse, the life of the driver compared to a boat and its skipper, is 1 to 500 in favor of the boat. The harness and wagon, with its pins, buckles, straps, &c., make 350 chances against you, and the kinks in the horse's disposition count 150 more. Now my boat, and all her traps, ropes, oars, rowlocks, with me in charge, is free from all risk, excepting my falling overboard by over-drinking that old Grenada—and you may hunt down the ages to come for that proof. Yes, yes! It is my hobby to fish, and yet I never sold a fish in my life. The surplus have gone to my neighbors.

If I ever wanted 25 pounds and upwards of striped bass, or 10 pounds and upwards of blue fish, I just took a trip to Cuttyhunk or Montauk Point, anchored outside the breakers and threw into the surf. I seldom failed at either place. If it was 60 to 100 pounds of drum fish, take the first of the flood at Townsend's Inlet, stop with Wm. Doolittle at South Seaville, by Cape May and Millville R. R. from Camden. If it was mackerel, just ingratiate yourself into the good graces of a smack skipper at New York or New London, and before night I could have sufficient fun for the day, and harbor at night. But don't you sleep aboard, or, in other words, don't try it. Oh, no, don't; for their bunks are always full . . . Fire Island by L. I. R. R. to Babylon. Splendid quarters at "Snediker's House." He or his successor will cater for a fisherman's wants and charter "Capt. John" and his Block Island built dory (always use your own gear), and if you want smooth water he will take you down to

Fire Island Inlet, where it is always so, or, if you want it
rough, he will (if your sea legs are good), give you a run
outside, where you will find from 1st of June, 10 to 12-
pound blue fish. In two hours, with the same good skipper, your humble servant hauled in over 1000 pounds,
and weighing from 7 to 15 pounds each. But you want
leather cots on two fingers and thumb of each hand or
you will sigh for home. And then, again, at the same
place, on the 1st to 20th of October, the fish are well fed
and bound south to winter, but they always stop in this
inlet just to clean it out of all the bait; and it is done
pretty quickly. Use a metal jig and heavy linen cod
line. The landlord will put up a good snack and send a
carriage to and from the dory. It is the cleanest, neat-
est fishing in the world. We never unhook the rascals.
They can beat you at that game. You just throw the
ravenous critter into the boat, line and all. These boats
are roomy and smart. Take plenty of good cigars;
Capt. John likes them, if you don't.

If you want a shorter trip, try it at Watch Hill for
five pounds and upwards blue fish. You must always
have good sea legs on for outside fishing. It is well to
run Narraganset Beach, wind off shore, with a long trail
for blue fish. Take the harpoon along for an occasional
sword fish. Off New London harbor you can generally
get good fun, and if you fail you can buy of other boats
at a cheap rate and take the Shore Line R. R. home
three times a day. Your friends need not put you under
oath as to the " silver hooks," and New Londoners never
peach on their customers.

Reader—I have a desire that you should try your luck
at Montauk Point, with a heavy squid as before men-

tioned, and if it is a failure you just go on the beach
outside, facing the Atlantic, ten rods or more from the
light, make the better end of your line fast above high
water mark, coil up your line for a long throw, follow
the receding comber, and before he comes rolling back
send the squid outside the second sea; then up the bank
for your life, and I will insure you a 15-pound weak fish,
or a blue fish of the same size. But you must do it
early in October. Here let me say that you will have no
difficulty in finding a home with the keeper. I never
knew a real genuine fisherman to be refused hospitality
in such places. I never knew a mean, purse-proud, stingy
fisherman. I have tried it from Cape May to Nantucket,
including Long Island Sound; from New Haven to Montauk Point, both on the main and island side, and always
found good quarters, not forgetting Plum Gut or Gard-
ner's Bay. A real fisherman is a true philosopher. If
the fish won't bite he always sees a reason for it, and you
never find him mixed up with a parcel of larks who are
always ready for fun, and, like the dog in the manger,
"neither fish nor cut bait." The fisherman is ready to
take any quarters offered him. He never ridicules the
look of the table cloth or the soiled apron of the hostess;
never leaves his fishing boots in the sitting room, nor
asks the price of board. If he has two or three real
genuine cronies who have been tried in the piscatorial
scales, who understand the ropes, not given to drink, or
grumbling under any circumstances, and who never
"stow away bait" or refuse to "pull kelleck" when ordered, and who never mutiny or tell family secrets, then
the landlord is ready to respond to your request to go
a-fishing. But, if otherwise, he "shuts pan" on all appli-

cations for that voyage. I would not go fishing with a promiscuous set of people any sooner than I would steal bait.

I got my foot in that kind of mud once, and that will answer for life.

It was made up that we should charter a Greenport smack for a week's fishing. Stores were laid in freely at New Haven, sweethearts and wives all kissed, and we on our way down Sound. The craft could scarcely stow away in bunks three persons beside the skipper and boy, much less the dozen " wild cats " that we numbered. Sleep was out of the question. The toddy stick danced in the glasses. The small stores were hoggishly strewed about the cabin and decks. The skipper had orders to run for Shagwanna Reef. The wind was light from the westward and the tide ebb. The noise in the cabin was being quieted down. I said to the skipper, "It is now about daylight. I know the way down Sound, and, as we have cut off your sleep, suppose you get a nap; but leave the boy with me and we will call you if necessary." The old man crawled into the hold at the side of the well, boots and clothes all on (nautically, " all standing "), and in five minutes snored loud and deep. We were down abreast of Faulkner's Island at sunrise, with barely steering way on her. I made a confidant of my little companion, took a good long warp, made fast to the small boat, gave the boy 50 cents, sheared the smack close inside of " Light House Rock," jumped into the small boat, gave her a shear, and landed safely without a jar to the smack or boat. The little chap hauled his wind, and down Sound he went. The dog, " Watch," rightly named, was on guard, raising the question of trespass, and forbade my crawling up the bank. This brought out the family, with the good, kind Eli Kimberly at the lead. He called the dog off, bade me come up and report myself. I did so and gave him my name, adding that the smack yonder had a jolly set of boys on board, bound down Sound on a fishing frolic, and that I had mutinied, and for the trespass committed by landing on his island, I craved his forgiveness. I was introduced to his family, called in to a splendid breakfast, my story told with considerable satisfaction, in that I was so suddenly transferred from a " hell on earth," to a cluster of souls congenial in every respect, and here began an intimacy and friendship that was bright and warm till the day of his death. On this island, which lies abreast of Guilford, five miles from the main, I found splendid fishing among the reefs and rocks, and with the old patriarch and his family always found a welcome. When he resigned his responsibilities on the island, he very kindly gave me an introduction to Capt. Oliver N. Brooks, his successor, and I was highly honored by being installed into his beautiful and happy family, with whom I have ever since received a happy welcome. God bless them all.*

The writer, until within three years has had glorious fishing at this island through the kindness and direction

---

* Faulkner's Island Light was established by the Government in 1801. It has had but four different keepers. Eli Kimberly occupied that position 33 years and was succeeded by Capt. Oliver N. Brooks, Nov. 18, 1851, and the same gentleman is yet in charge. Of its early keepers I have no data. The island is fast reducing in length and breadth by reason of gales. I consider Home Fishing here and vicinity better than I have ever found, and the hospitality extended me off and on for 30 years by both families is without its parallel.

of both Mr. Kimberly and his successor, Mr. Brooks, in company with Uncle Fred. Lines, his nephew Augustus E. Lines, and Eli Kimberly, 2d, and we sometimes discussed the adventures over an annual dinner, at which time the poet tried his hand for a few verses, of which those which presently follow were counted the best. Death has made an inroad among us and the old patriarch, Eli Kimberly, Esq., and our bosom friend Uncle Fred. Lines, the jolly Good Samaritan, have both been called from our ranks, and are waiting in the grave for the second coming of him whom they both loved and served faithfully. Our harps are on the willows; our ranks are broken; we mourn their loss, and " but a little longer stay" ourselves.

The present occupant of Faulkner's Island, Capt. Oliver N. Brooks, like his predecessor, is a humane, kind-hearted gentleman, a perfect boatman and a Christian; the family, a pattern for the world; and the world will say "Amen" to my assertion. They are all adapted to the position,—with a " Grace Darling " among them who can aid the father in cases of shipwreck on those rocky surroundings, or as gently touch the keys of a piano, or the violin strings as any professor of music. And if a sudden emergency should arise requiring a broiler or a chowder, she can take the boat and catch and clean the fish just as neatly as the father can; but neither of them would expect to catch a game fish with the wind to the eastward. Salt water fishermen will please take note.

And now for the poetry, thought to be " sum punkins " when introduced, and extolled wonderfully by those present at the table. The author began to think it did

have some merit, but as he cast his eye around the table
and remembered that every soul present, including the
ladies, was admitted by the city at large to be much
better judges in piscatorial matters than poetry, he felt
more like taking his hat and cigar and retiring from the
thunders of applause that were tendered.   For who ever
knew a No. 1 master of a ship to be a good merchant?
or a fisherman a good poet?   It is not in the nature of
things.   Therefore, I promise to be found in the piscatorial ranks all the rest of my days.   It is a trade I gave
particular attention to all through life from five years
old and upwards (began at the creek which in 1810 was
navigable for my "dug out" from the sea to Grand st.,
in New Haven), and will probably be closed out at Short
Beach, Branford.

TO ELI KIMBERLY, ESQ., OF GUILFORD.

FROM HIS FRIEND C. F. H.

In Eighteen Hundred Sixty-four, 'twas June,—
I think the thirteenth day, not far from noon;
'Twas early in the week, I well remember ;—

Three men with carpet bags well lined,
Emerged from State street with anxiety to find
The Shore Line road that leads down East,
Where lives a hero whose locks are bleached.

A council they had held for weeks
With Beckwith, whom everybody seeks
If they intend a voyage to make,
Where tides or winds or moons dictate.

The elder of the three was tall and slim,—
I'm sure there is no mistaking him;
We call him "Good Samaritan."
Ask all the poor within this region.

He always wears about his neck,
Both when he sleeps and when awake,
A white cravat,—it is his custom;
And he's often taken for a Parson.

The other two were younger men,
The elder, past two score and ten;
We often see him loud in clamor,
As he drops his auction hammer.

'Twas said in early days of him,
That by his name, he sure was kin
To Hotchkiss, whom you well remember,
Stole all the sheep away up yonder.

I knew him well when quite a youngster,
He always was inclined to wander;
He was a wicked, independent chap—
O how the master whaled his back!

I've known him when but quite a boy,
To rob hen-roosts and e'en destroy
Every old maid's cat within a mile,
And sell the skins for quite a pile.

But why detain you longer, friends?
We'll leave the youngster in his sins,
And pray by the help of God, he may
Reform and be a man some day.

But to my story.   And where's the last
Of these three gents who walked so fast
That one would think them on a wager,
Or else had drank their full of lager?

He was younger than the other men,
And by attention to his trade, when
Engravers were either fast asleep or tired,
Accomplished twice as much as men that's hired.

He was active, thorough and up betimes,
A habit quite peculiar to the Lines,
For he and " Uncle Fred." could shoot
Full twenty rods and kill a coot.

Well, off they started down the street,
Their tickets paid, each one seat,
To Guilford, in the Nutmeg State,
Where Eli third had dug the bait.

From the depot where the cars do meet,
I saw them start for Harbor street,
Where lives our friend and his good wife,
Away-from all that tends to strife.

Favored man, to have so kind a wife,
To sooth the sorrows of a declining life!
'Tis beautiful, indeed, thus hand in hand,
To cheer each onward to the promised land.

But to my story, and then to bed,
To dream of fish hooks, " lines " and lead,
Old Faulkner, too, must have a share,
Unless thrown out by " Old Nightmare."

At last the morning came, 'twas bright and clear,
The sun not up but mighty near ;
The wind was light, about South-west,
The breakfast one of Madam's best.

Well, there was Minnie, that good boat,
As good as if made of solid oak ;
She turned her head about South-west,
And away she sped to do her best.

2

Old Faulkner, she was there in sight,
Goose Island, too, loomed up quite bright,
North-rocks, three-quarter, also, by reason of the ebb,
Had just begun to show their head.

"Ease off the sheet," the old man roared,
"The wind is free, haul up the board!
Head her for the wharf, stand by your line,
Let's call on 'Brooks,' and save the fine."

And now the "permit" kindly granted,
Winkles bagged, the wharf inspected,
Fish hooks sharpened, kelleck ready,
Away they went for outer Stony.

And then to work with hooks all bright,
The fish are coming left and right;
"Ba!" says the old man, "what's the matter,
With Uncle Fred, in such a splatter?"

"First fish!" my boy, and such a lounder,
As Eli hauled an awful flounder;
"Ha! it don't count," rung in the air
As Hotchkiss hauled a pretty pair.

"Now go it, Gussy, that's the kind,
Don't loose him, play him, give him line."
"Hurrah for Uncle Fred!" one said,
As in he hauled a hook and lead.

"Come, it's time to car," the old man said,
"Let's save the fish before they're dead;
We counted in an awful number,
Including the skipper's line and sinker.

"Hurrah!" the whole boat's crew did cry,
As in the stern sheets they could spy
The old rat hauling by the pair
Another line,—he always has a spare.

"Hurrah! Hurrah! the boat! the boat!
"They cried," she'll never float
With all these fish, let's kelleck pull;
"By Jingo! it's true she's nearly full."

Poor Minnie, as she started in,
With all this precious load of sin,
With fish well stowed in every nook,
She seemed to whisper, "Who's high hook?"

Now all good people on the Bay
As Minnie turned her head that way,
Came looking in her, every nook,
And cried aloud, "Who's high hook?"

The old man, then, with face all bright,
His left eye squint, his mouth all right,
Replied, "My friend, this is no fiction,
For Hotchkiss catches all creation."

So now, old friend, I send the jacket,
To keep you dry amid the racket;
My prayers to God shall never cease
That in Paradise we meet in peace.

If the reader is inclined for a fare of black fish, with
an occasional sea bass, he should try old "Shagwanna,"
--the East end on the ebb tide, and West on the flood.
The reef lies inside of Montauk Point on the island side.
You need a hand lead line in case the Rip shows itself.
With small lobster and good sized clams for bait you
can't miss them, say two hours on the ebb through slack
water and one hour flood. You can get to it from New
London, Sag Harbor, or Plum Gut. If you are not shortened for time, try it in the Race with three hooks about
half an hour on the low-water slack. It will pay you,

sure. In the month of October, you should go to Greenport or Sag Harbor, pick out a good boat and skipper,
the latter smart, kindly disposed, and not too proud to
dig your bait; not too wise on national matters; not too
talkative; not a rum sucker, nor a harum-scarum, swearing braggadocio, but a good, quiet gentleman, one who
knows sufficient to take good care of his wife, boat and
passenger. Rig yourself out with a good set of "oilers,"
and never start out with the wind east. I say again,
take your own gear, a small basket of "snack," and a
good jack-knife in your pocket. Hand fishing, remember,
all through this country. But, to sum up the fishing
(and I have worked at it more or less for more than a half
century), get the acquaintance of the King of Faulkner's
Island, Capt. O. N. Brooks and family; carry good cre-
dentials; wait on yourself; learn the tides and the rocks;
get him to show you "Sharp Rock" (Stony Island Reef),
"North Rocks," Shepherd's Rock, "Old Table" (well
baited up), "Outer ledge," on North Reef, East Reef,
etc., etc., and if you don't thank me for the suggestion
I shall put you down as a person possessing neither good
judgment or entitled to the cognomen of a fisherman.
But don't be mean when you shake hands to part, and if
he won't take it, put it under your plate.

A good fisherman never can be small or mean if he
tries.

One more : If by stress of weather you are driven off
shore, you just shape your course for this island. You
can make a lee any time, and once within his jurisdiction
you will rejoice that you are shipwrecked, for the Captain
and every soul on the island each have hearts as big as
an ox. It would not distress the writer if some day

while he is fishing at the "Cow and Calf," off Short
Beach in his little eight-foot dingey, he should lose his
row-locks and both oars, wind blowing a hurricane N.W.,
and be driven down Sound; for if I had Faulkner's
Island under my lee, I would sing and whistle "Hail,
Columbia, happy land," all the way down to the island
and shoot the dingey into his harbor, where many a
"greenhorn" or shipwrecked crew have found shelter
and a welcome from the storm. And further, it would
not be a very bitter pill to take if, after hauling the little
dingey up on the beach, I should get fog-bound for a
week. It is one of the best places for a real genuine,
genteel fisherman on the coast. Of course my reader
will understand the requisite qualifications to enable him
to enter into all the privileges of this beautiful home,
and enjoy fishing to his heart's content. But where is
my text? "A rolling stone gathers no moss." Let us
see how this will apply to the author during his life.
"Experience is the best schoolmaster," and it is generally
admitted that those who have this schooling are the
safest parties to impart advice.

At twelve years old, at the New Township Academy,
New Haven, corner of Chapel and Academy streets, the
author graduated with sixty others by defacing the school
room and driving the master out and up Chapel street.
This was my last schooling. [It was my fault, and not
of my good kind parents.] I smuggled myself on board
a whale ship lying in the cove at New Haven, and on
the third day was caught and sent ashore. At thirteen
I went to sea by consent of parents with Capt. Peter
Storer, and followed up that life till twenty-two years
old. Married and went into merchandise, and afterwards

as special sheriff at Rochester, N. Y. Returned to New
Haven; ran a coaster to Albany; moved to New York;
merchandised eleven years or more; returned to New
Haven; next packed beef in Illinois; moved to Ohio
and packed butter and pork; returned to New Haven;
opened an auction room on Chapel st.; ran it two years;
gained sufficient for a good outfit for California; returned
and opened another butter store in New Haven, and
afterward moved to Kansas; returned to New Haven;
worked hard; began to pick up the crumbs by the aid
of Gerard Hallock, built a good house corner of Columbus
and Liberty streets, well furnished and paid for it; made
an asylum for all good pilgrims; feasted them and their
friends; always kept "two upper chambers," like the
Shunamite woman, for the men of God, without regard
to sect, age, or condition; opened a large auction room
on State st.; drove it night and day; got tired; closed
it out in six years; made $22,000; wife sick with asthma;
moved to Vineland, N. J., invested $8,000, fenced a farm,
with a nice cottage, where I could in a few hours take a
run down to Cape May and fish. Could not get sufficient
off the farm to support the family; changed the farm for
property in Philadelphia; made other shifts, but the final
result was a loss. Returned to New Haven with the
body of a kind, good wife, who had shared in these ups
and downs of life, without a murmur or complaint. Had
sufficient capital for any reasonable business; put in
$10,000 in real estate, reserving sufficient for an auction
business. Ran the latter two years, but the business
was spoiled or else the writer was, and wound it up, the
former a total loss—and every other piece of real estate
met the same result. But I never whine nor grumble.

So, one day, seated in my old arm chair, reviewing the past scenes of life, I came to the conclusion that "A roll-stone gathers no moss." One word now on friends. If you succeed by hard knocks to get a little of the ready, you may be sure that FRIENDS will be after it. It is your bosom FRIENDS that you need to fear. It may be your case as in mine, those " with whom you walk together to the House of God." If you have not the courage to say NO when these friends apply for your endorsement, go home and ask counsel of your wife; after this, should you decide to give him your name, for God's sake don't endorse beyond your ability to pay, and then do it like a man, without the aid of the Bankrupt Law. I thank God that I never went through that gate, though it was enacted for the honest man. The time was when men's word was as good as their bond, and endorsers were protected; but now "men are truce breakers," "incontinent and liars." The "truth is not in them." Remember that if you lend your name, you lose your money and your friend both.

Ecclesiasticus is truthful when he says, "Many a thing was lent them, reckoned it to be found, and put them to trouble that helped them." " Till he hath received he will kiss a man's hand, and for his neighbor's money he will speak submissively; but when he should repay he will prolong the time, return words of grief and complain of the time; many, therefore, have refused to lend for other men's ill dealings, fearing to be defrauded. Suretyship hath undone many of good estate and shaken them as the waves of the sea, mighty men hath it driven from their houses so that they wandered among strange nations. But—forgive thy neighbor the hurt he hath done thee. So shall thy sins be forgiven thee when thou prayest."

Now a few words of advice to inexperienced fishermen. Approach a spot where others are engaging in the same amusement with great caution and stillness. Give your neighbor a good berth, and never drop your boat over his fishing ground. Never slam your "kelleck" over, but guide it carefully to the bottom, and as she tails to the tide or wind, be sure that the boat swings clear of your neighbor. Always carry a good long warp that you may carefully drop down over new ground. If your neighbor is successful, don't disturb him with noise or movement of any kind. Fish can hear better than you can (old philosophy to the contrary notwithstanding), and by reckless movements you drive the fish off from any small reef. In a quiet day I can drive a shoal of porpoises out of our bay by a few taps on the gunwale of my boat; but if I am on a reef of small dimensions and do this, I may as well up kelleck, go home and fish in the well as to expect a black fish or sea bass to take the hook for a half hour. Do you purposely enter a trout stream through brush heaps and wood-choppers? No; you approach that stream on tip-toe, lest the game should be alarmed. Well, apply the same care in your operations with salt water fish, otherwise you never will be " high hook " in that region. When I get a shoal of blue or weak fish around my boat I seal my lips and " throw stosh " till the last; and, if they break off short and suddenly, I know it's all up in that location. The shark or porpoise drove them off, or the same result by a passing boat or the change of tide. If I was a young man, inclined to fish from a boat, I would as soon rob an old fisherman of his toddy as to disturb him while he is fishing. Then give him a good berth and see that the sin of disturbing him while in the enjoyment of his occupation don't lay at your door. Take no loud talkers with you in your boat. Do as I do, better go alone, with a conscience void of offence toward God or man. But, above all things, don't disturb anybody in fishing, and then, if called upon to explain, throw yourself on your dignity and tell the old man to help himself, for "the waters are free to all." I have heard this too much. "Ye are my witnesses." I believe that a soul guilty of this crime of disturbing an old fisherman is as liable to be lost as for theft.

And now, when you can't find a better place on the shore to summer and fish, come to my boarding house, Short Beach, Branford, Conn.; stages three times a day, from New Haven. Price of board, $10.00 a week. Open June 1st to November.

A VOYAGE UP THE MEDITERRANEAN.

Foot of Wall street, New York—1000 people on the Dock—Fasts
singled—Strange interference—Wild scenes in James st.—New life
to surrounding—Skipper cries "Let go."—Pilot assumes his duties
—Mutiny—Sam the cook—Signal for off Pilot—Stand by for Pilot
boat—Farewell—Bang went the Carronade—Put her E. S. E.—
Sealing in Massafuro—Off Western Islands—"Ize no 'lijah, Massa"
—Sam's faith—A Ship's Spar—Sea Bass weighing 25 lbs. each—
The boy high hook—Sam's Chowder—Rev. Goodell—Shark and his
Pilot—Boy victorious—Rushing scenes on deck—Sam's soliloquy on
Turtle—Jim Cook overboard—Whistling for a Breeze—Whirrah!
for a spanking Breeze—Shaped course for Cape St. Vincent—At
anchor in Gibraltar Bay—Nations under tribute to Gibraltar—Siege
of Gibraltar—Moorish Jew and petit Senorita—Departure for Malta
—Wonderful escape off Mount Stromboli—A Levanter—Honor to
whom Honor is due—Rub and Go is a good Pilot—Quarantine mum-
mery—Sam's away down in Dixy—Men hanging in chains—Turkey
Buzzards—St. Paul's Church at Malta—Napoleon's Raid—Smoke
House at Lazaretta—Knights of Malta and Jerusalem—Ancient City
of Mileta—St. Paul's Cave—Ladrone of the Ancient City—Hard
Fight on the Marina—Sam to the rescue—Departure for Sicily—
Mount Ætna—20,000 people on the Marina—Earthquake at Messina
—Inspection of Ætna by the author and Commodore Elisha Peck,
of New Haven—History by ancient Authors—93,000 people de-
stroyed—Adieu to Sicily—Homeward Bound with 80 sail of Vessels
—A severe Gale—Sam again a Hero—Many a slip between the cup
and the lip—Vessel on her beam ends—Cowardice of Sailors—
Skipper a Host! read it, read it, for the author cannot do the sub-
ject justice—" Ye cowards, you! try the pumps and go below till I

call you "—Continuous Gale—Soundings off Chincoteage Shoal—
Codfish plenty—Blown off the Coast three times—Anchored in the
Horse Shoe—Author's life again saved by Sam when knocked off
main yard; never born to be drowned.

FIFTY-SIX years ago the neat little full-rigged brig
Shepherdess, owned by Hotchkiss & Harrison, of
New Haven, formerly a crack Charleston packet, under
Capt. Bill Lines, but in 1822 in charge of Capt. Peter
Storer, who is now resting on his laurels in his
own Snug Harbor at Westville, full fourscore years
and seven, hale and hearty, a true gentleman and
a genuine old salt,—lay at the dock foot of Wall
street, New York, bound to the Mediterranean, having
on board Revs. Goodell and Bird with their wives,
for the Palestine Mission, and to be landed at Malta.
Everything about the little craft was neat and tidy as a
man-of-war,—topsails sheeted home, fasts singled, and a
large concourse of people on the dock to bid adieu to
missionaries, with the usual number of dock wallopers
without any particular object in view. The wind strong
N. W. over the city, the tide just on the ebb, the skipper
and pilot stood on the quarter-deck in the wake of the
main rigging, and your humble servant at the wheel,
where the former cast an eye as if to learn whether that
post was filled, and seemingly just ready to nudge the
pilot that all was ready, when a great commotion was
seen on the dock. A colored man in full speed, swing-
ing his hat, running, crying " Hold on! Hold on! Captain." (A singular interference certainly.) " What do
you want?" cried the skipper, as he stretched his head
over the crowd of people. " Stop a minute, Captain!"
came from the messenger, as he made his way through

the throng and placed one foot on the wharf log, caught his breath, and, pointing to the cook who sat in the door of his " galley," " Here, you, Jim Butterfield, come ashore! Your old woman is dying in New Haven. Come ashore, dis minit! I'se telling you de trufe; don't you go dis vige. Jump ashore, Jim! Yuse got a baby, Jim and—"

We heard no more, but the shouts of the people and dive that the old cook made for the dock was a splendid scene for an artist, for he grasped the hand of the messenger, jumped the rail, and up the dock they went, and he, like a faithful husband, left all his dunnage behind, the vessel without a cook, not even saying to the skipper " by your leave, sir." Capt. Peter had stood in his usual position with a smile more of pity than anger. Casting his eye aloft he spanned all the surroundings, while the little craft, like a high-spirited horse, was chafing as the wind gave an increased pressure to the canvass and bid fair to part her fastenings or carry away her spars. He turned to the mate, Mr. Alfred Thomas, brother of our ex-Postmaster, L. A. Thomas, Esq., and said, " Put the main-royal in the beckets, settle down the topsails and topgallant sails, clew up the courses, furl the jib and stay-sail!" and, like a true philosopher as he was a true sailor, turned his eye to the dock, where stood a number of colored men, and said, " Which of you boys will ship as cook? $18.00 a month, about six months, and up the Mediterranean? Who speaks first?" when I heard a clear, musical voice as though from a speaking trumpet, ring out from between two large, broad, thick red lips, and I traced the sound to a long, lank Maryland-looking darkey, who stood leaning on a dock spile, his body six

feet two high, with a happy smile on his countenance,
large white eyes, body well dressed, clean white linen
collar reaching to his ears, an umbrella and whip in his
hand, apparently about " three sheets in the wind," or,
as an Englishman would say, " 'arf and 'arf;" but somehow I was favorably struck with the man, especially as
the reply to the skipper came ricochetting through my
ears—" I'll go, sar." " Well," says Capt. Peter, " where's
your dunnage?" " Dase be up to James street, sar."
" How long will it take to get them and yourself back
here?" " Jes' a few minits, sar!" And the captain
turned to me and said: " Boy, you take this darkey and
in just one hour return him with his dunnage, and plant
him in the caboose."

No more words were necessary. I dropped the wheel,
jumped on the rail, reached out my hand, clasped that
of the darkey, and made a good nice ten-foot leap of it
and landed partly on my feet and in his arms, and as
we gathered for a run I looked up in his shining black
face and asked his name. " My name be's Sam Chace,
massa," was the reply, and away we went. I chartered
a dray at the head of the dock, turned up South st. to
Burling slip, turned into Water st., while the great long-
spliced Sam had a death-like grip on the forward rung
of the cart, and both my arms around his waist, and we
went John Gilpin like over the stones to James st., where
we were dumped. Sam had an eye to business, as he
sprang for a gate-way, into a side-yard full of clothes
and clothes lines, up an outside stairs, through a trap
door, which opened into an old dilapidated ball room,
where " those that dance must pay the fidler." Half a
dozen colored females were smoking off the fumes of

rum, "looking like the sad effects of a misspent day." But Sam did not stop here. I sighted him as he straddled over a vacancy in the flooring, down a pair of stairs into a grocery fronting on a lane. It may truly be said "a stern chase is a long chase." Sam's walking stilts were useful as well as ornamental, but he could beat the wind. He steered straight to the bar, slammed in a fair good-sized drink from a decanter, got it to his mouth just in time for me to "cork him," and he took it like a philosopher, threw down the glass and sung out in a very commanding tone, "Here, landlord! gin me half gallon rum and two pounds sugar; leve 'em be in de measure till I want um. And here, you Jane! go dis minit get my duds. I'se going to sea in fifteen minits wid dis here childers." And the wail that went up from the dozen women present was truly heart-rending. Jane exclaimed, "Now Sam, duz yuse mean de trufe—youze goang to sea?" But there was no time for argument or reason. The news of Sam's departure went through the neighborhood and in five minutes we had a large concourse of both males and females,—some on barrels, boxes, broken chairs, and many that could only lean—the whole scene, including the bar, forming a portion of a circle was lively in the extreme, Sam standing in a position commanding a view of the whole. The landlord, as ordered, put in two quarts more of rum in the measure, each but the hero drinking freely, Jane just entering the door with Sam's duds, when our hero threw down two dollars on the bar, grabbed Jane by the waist with a kiss, took up the gallon measure and gave the contents a circular flirt over the whole audience, exclaiming, "Here, you brack darters of Adam, take de balance on it and get sober

agin I come back." Not a drop did Sam take, but, turning to me with a lively expression of pleasure, said,
" Now, Massa Charley, I'se ready to go." And, amid the
roar of laughter of some, and the wailing of others, we
turned our faces, found the carman at his post. " Off"
was the orders. Turned into South st., made rather a
crooked wake, but a safe landing at the foot of Wall st.
Found the wind still N. W., a thousand people on the
dock, paid the carman two dollars, installed Sam in the
galley inside of fifty minutes.

A new life came to the surroundings. The pilot wiped
the ashes from his cigar, the skipper assumed the weather
quarter-deck and said, " Mr. Thomas, let go clue lines,
buntlines and down haul; sheet home; up both topsails,
topgallant sails. Here, boy ! throw the main royal out
of the beckets; up spanker; clear away jib and stay-
sail down-hauls; run them both up. What do you say
up there, boy ?" and the answer " Hoist away, sir," came
warbling back from the topgallant crosstrees through a
cracked voice just on the change. " Clear the spanker
sheets; let the boom shake till we get the true wind."
And " Are you ready, Mr. Thomas ?" " Aye, sir," was
the reply, "All ready, sir." And as I slipped down the
main-topgallant back stays without touching a rattling,
the skipper turned to me and said, " Boy, take the
wheel," and in the same breath, the mate by a signal
cried "All ashore that's going ! In gang plank ! Stand
by your lines !" when the skipper, in his sweet musical
voice, cried "Let go !" Cheer upon cheer went up from
the shore and neighboring shipping, off went our carronade, whose muzzle stuck over the taffrail, and the
skipper in his quiet, gentlemanly way, tipped his hat to

the audience on shore, and turning to the pilot gave him the command.

With the full strength of the ebb tide and cracking breeze the little craft, with head pointed down stream, " walked the waters like a thing of life," and seemed to say—Clear the track. I have no time to lose; the precious work in hand is to carry glad tidings to the people of Palestine, and like Nehemiah of old in building the walls of Jerusalem, have no time to talk. Away, then, ye Sanbalets, Tobiahs, and Gershoms, for " why should the work cease whilst I leave it and come down to you?" Place no obstructions in my way. God furnishes the wind that wafts us on our voyage, and not one feeble " cat's paw " must be lost.

"Starboard!" cried the pilot. "So—steady that—steady, sir," was the reply, and if the boy did not show pride he certainly felt it in his boots, doing an able seaman's duty on his third voyage, at fifteen years of age. The skipper sat on the weather cable box, smoking a splendid Havana of his own manufacture, a silent observer, with an eye aloft occasionally, measuring in his own mind the full strength of spars, back-stays and canvas. The pilot stood in the wake of the main rigging, his eye reaching under the leach of the foresail, and over the weather cat-head, and turning to the skipper said, " Captain, she goes like a scalded hog, and plump ten knot an hour. Is your standing rigging good?" and before the reply came, the little brig, pressed by a real good puff of wind, stuck her nose into a combing "tide rip," and took the water in through both hawse holes. I never knew what reply the skipper made, but he turned to me with a twinkle in his eye and said, " Boy, do you want

3

any help at the wheel?" "None, sir; for she steers like
a duck," was the reply, and the old man knew it; for the
voyage previous he and myself, "trick-a-trick" scud her
twenty-two hours through a real tearing gale of wind,
and not another hand touched the wheel.   That was on
a voyage home from Malaga, Isaac English, mate, and
sick below.   But let us turn to the scenes around us, for
they began to be interesting.   The flood tide had met us
in the Narrows, and with it the old roll of the Atlantic.
The wind still freshened and wore westerly.   All the light
kites were in the beckets and gaskets.   The four missionaries had passed below under the usual premonitions of
sea-sickness.   The crew, partly "mops and brooms,"
were growling with the mate about the usual rations of
grog, he thinking they would expect, as was the custom
then, to have grog passed when taking "distance and
departure," and if the wind held that event would soon
take place.   Good, kind-hearted man, he was fearful that,
come to add the fourth ration and the "sweethearts and
wives" in the course of another hour to what they had
when they left the dock, they might not be able to carry
the whole load without a fight.

Mr. Thomas was a young man, a Christian gentleman
and a genuine sailor, a man of resolution and gentleness,
withal, but if the case required action and could not be
adjusted without it, he could walk into treble his weight,
and the parties in interest would find themselves whipped
before they knew it,—much like our old friend R. S. P.
Well, the question was satisfactorily adjusted in less than
two minutes, and without its being known abaft the
mainmast, by his picking up the two ringleaders, dumped
them down the forecastle hatch and kept them there till

sober next morning. The usual rations were reserved till outside the Hook. Good for the mate. Now for Sam Chace, the cook, who during all this time had been drumming up his galley traps, scoured tins and coppers, mustered up towels, and everything was in apple-pie order, with a stream of smoke issuing from his galley equal to a Londonderry steamship, and had brought himself to an anchor in the weather door of his caboose, with his good sweet face peering out, having cast off his shore togs and mounted what he called his wedding rig,—a beautiful middy's cap on his head, trimmed with gold lace, marked over the front "Sobriety," worked on rich black velvet. His shirt collar of white linen before described, had given place to a clean blue man-of-war shirt, worked anchors on each lap of the collar, open in the throat, heavy No. 2 white duck pants, held up by the hips, a beautiful white linen handkerchief stuck in the pocket behind, a small silver comb back of his head, holding a long, curled Chinese cue, and a splendid pair of serge slippers, 12 size, sleeves rolled up, showing tattoo in Indian red ink, and a large dolphin on his breast. There he sat like a Prince of Timbuctoo, humming to himself in a low key "Away down in Dixey." Every thing inside his galley " shone like a negro's eye agin the moon." Ah, thinks I, here's music for the voyage. An extra lunch had been laid on the capstan head for the captain and pilot, a signal had been set for an off pilot boat and she was laying by for us about five miles off, and for which we were heading. The lunch was finished, the pilot assumed his former position, the wind had wore more westerly, the skipper had lighted a fresh cigar, when Sam in all his glory, with a cup of coffee and a

" slapper," on a tray stepped out of his galley, walked
straight up to the skipper, tipped his lace cap and pointing to me, still at the wheel, said, " Sar, wid your leave,
a cup of coffee for dat chicken, sar ?" and, as he received
a nod of assent, laid the traps over the binnacle, came
round under my lee and said, " Honey, you go dare and
' mungee,' it be hulsome for uze belly ; it warm you better
dan rum." And he put his feeler on the wheel as supple
as any old salt, whispering in my ear, " Hurry, child ! dis
pilot is going to lebe us." And I gave him the helm and
his course with as much confidence of his seamanship as
of his kind heart. The pilot boat, with jib to windward,
had launched his little dingey, then about half a mile
distant, and as I returned to my post Sam whispered
again, smoothing down his belly, " Dere, honey, dat is
good ! For when dis ere child is hungry, go way child !
go way ! but when my belly's full, a little child can play
wid me," and the old negro left me completely in his
favor, an affection planted on the dock at Wall st., and
nursed by almost continuous contact for a dozen years or
more, till his death. The pilot's duty had closed, and
our skipper resumed his charge, and standing on the
weather quarter his familiar voice came to the ear of all,
" Stand by for the pilot's small boat ! Port your helm !
Let her come easy, boy ! Stand by lee main braces !
Steady your helm ! Main topsail haul ! Round with
your yards ! So, belay that !" And in an instant the
pilot dropped into his little dingey, waving adieu and
pleasant voyage. The little brig had not lost her way.
Bang went the carronade as the skipper said, " Hard up
your helm ! Shiver the yards ! Meet her with your
helm ! Fill away main yards ! Steady, boy, steady !

How do you head now?" " S. W., sir," came the response. " Starboard a little, now what?" " S. by E., sir." " Put her E. S. E. and keep that course till further orders. Trim her at that, Mr. Thomas," and then " Come aft and we will take bearings and distance, and make up the watches for the voyage." It was now six P. M. The breeze held good, rate by log, nine knots. Watches were arranged, and my lot fell to the skipper. Long-spliced Jim Cook, of the mate's watch, relieved the helm, and the boy was soon in close confab with his new crony the cook, and as you have had considerable display of nautical phrases thus far, it will answer for the voyage, the remainder of the Journal will be devoted to incidents, historical, piscatorial, and amusing,—founded on fact, not fiction.

The starboard watch had the charge, and your humble servant with the skipper were pacing the main deck. The night was beautiful, the wind just abaft the beam, every stitch of canvas doing its duty, and the log at twelve denoted eight knots. The skipper said, " In 1802 I was in the ship Sally with my father, Capt. Nathaniel Storer, laying in Hell Gate harbor on the coast of Patagonia, gathering a cargo of seal. The weather was cold, the interior mountains full of snow, and at that season the seal would land at the shore and beach in great quantities, comprising the female with the young ' pompys ' at her side, and the male, called ' old wig.' The skin of the former was the object of our voyage, while the pompey was useless. The old wigs are not plenty, nor are their skins desirable, the covering being coarse hair and a mantle around his neck of long gray. They are all entirely harmless and show no disposition to de-

fend themselves, but will make for the water on the
approach of their captors; consequently their retreat is
cut off and they are easily killed by clubs. They may
be in rookeries of 50 or 500, and seldom but one old wig
seen in a rook. When a sufficient number are killed for
the day they are skinned, taking care of cutting the hide,
stretched on pegs, salted on board the ship, and, in this
case, 45,000 taken to Canton and sold for 87½ cents each.
The skinning process proceeds while the young pompys
are at the side of the mother crying piteously, and were
taken up by the lad. Our skipper petted and soothed
them like a young child. The sea lion is the male of the
old wig, of no use but for oil. They weigh 300 or 400
pounds, and our hero, having no duties to perform, spent
his time on shore riding on the backs of these creatures
and playing with the pompys or puppies."

The little craft had held the westerly wind, a light
leading breeze, the weather had been splendid thus far,
our passengers had put on their sea legs and were chat-
ting on the quarter deck, the crew had become sober, we
in a lovely climate and a smooth sea. By observation
we found ourselves in the vicinity of St. Michael, one of
the Azores or Western Islands, the wind nearly a calm,
surrounded with drift weed, and occasionally a green
turtle in sight, about 100 miles from land, and here, no
doubt, we were to remain a week or more, whistling for
a breeze. "Horse latitude, by Jingo!" exclaimed the
skipper, as he threw his old cap on the deck and called
Sam, the cook, aft and said, "How do you stand for fresh,
Sam?" "Well, sar, dere be no beef left sin' Sunday;
wese got 5 pair chicks, 15 ducks, 2 grunters and plenty
of de sarce, sar!" The skipper cast his eye in the wake

of the fore-rigging, put his spy-glass to his eye, turned to Sam and said, " Give us a real good, rich fish chowder for dinner; put in plenty of pork and port wine, and be ready with your dinner when we get the sun at meridian." Sam rolled up his eyes in amazement, and exclaimed, "I'se no 'lijah, Massa ! I'se got no fish, dis child can't make fish ? can't make chowder widout fish, Massa !" " Never you mind, Sam, get your potatoes and pork sliced, and in half an hour you shall have fish; you want faith, Sam." The cook went forward in wonder, soliloquizing as he went. The skipper knew where the fish were, and sang out, " Stand by there on the forecastle with a line, and get a running bowline round that spar, just under the lee bow." And sure enough, there were the fish. The water was black with sea bass which had been feeding on barnacles attached to the spar, apparently a large ship's mast, broken below the hounds and about twenty feet long. The barnacles were of the clam species, about two inches long, and completely encased the spar. The prize was dropped astern. The fish, though a little disturbed at first, soon became reconciled to the situation, and returned to the spar. It was a sight for a lifetime, the water being black with real genuine sea bass, weighing from 5 to 25 pounds, and a thousand in number. If Sir Izaak Walton, or Sam Drake, of Rochester, could have witnessed that scene there would have been some tall expressions, though the former, it is said, never swore an oath in his life. Sea bass of 2 to 8 pounds, caught inside of Montauk Point are counted, for broiling and chowder, the best salt water fish. The male is distinguished by bright, variable brown and blue shades. But let us return to the scene on deck. The skipper was throwing the grains and the mate the harpoon, and the fish were coming right and left, while your humble servant, never without good gear, used the hook and line, and the water being clear and fish near the surface, he could take his pick of size. The officers mutilated their fish, while the hook and line brought them on deck in all their beauty and glory, and besides, the youngster came off high hook. We had about thirty fish on deck, when the skipper ordered the prize to be cast off, adding, "we have all the fish we can care for. It is wicked to have them spoil." Sam was, of course, on hand for a fish, and had cut the throat of the skipper's first, weighing about eight pounds, and as your humble servant hauled in a 24-pounder Sam fastened to him as he struck the deck, and exclaimed, " Massa Charley, I'se got faith now, our skipper is a prophetum. I juss takes dis big fellow, cos he's a cracker for de chowder, and de tutherun for broil." And when the officers had taken the sun at meridian, Sam walked into the cabin with an immense kettle of chowder, that by its savory smell would tempt Queen Victoria or make Izaak Walton laugh both sides of his mouth, and having served the cabin he filled the forecastle kids, and we had a meal delicious and long to be remembered. The whole affair was a splendid ovation, commenced without faith and closed on time, agreeable to orders. And here is Sam's recipe for the chowder:

Put the iron kettle on a slow fire, of a capacity sufficient for your family.

> Put in a layer of clear sliced salt pork.
> Put in a layer of clear cuts of fish,
>   free from bone as possible.
> Put in a layer of clear sliced potatoes.
> Water to cover, only.

Repeat the three layers twice, after which one pound butter, pepper and salt to suit. Pour in one pint brandy, one pint catsup, one pint port wine, the juice of six lemons (fresh). Then, for the purpose of knowing when done, put three good sized potatoes on top. No pilot bread or crackers in the kettle, but they should be toasted, stewed in butter and served separate. No meal or flour, don't burn, nor forget the lemons.

Serve the chowder from the kettle, unless you have extra large platters. Fish cuts should be tied in muslin.

But the calm still prevailed, and all the whistling we could muster would not bring a breeze. The following day was Sunday, and at 10 A. M. all hands were called aft for religious services. Sermon from Rev. Mr. Goodell. Weather hot, made hardly tolerable by an awning over quarter deck. Several green turtle in sight on the surface. Saw a large shoal of right whale going west, apparently in a fight with several large threshers. Porpoises in shoals were turning feats amusing and certainly interesting, and it seemed as though the water was full of fish. A large shark made his appearance on our quarter, about fifty rods off, and as the four o'clock watch was relieved the author set to work for a more intimate acquaintance with him. I rigged out a good hook and line, baited with sea bass. The vessel had barely steerage way on her, and before night had coaxed the rascal within perhaps six rods, but he declined the hook. I noticed that in throwing any floating substance toward him that a small fish would dart out from his left side, examine the article and return to the shark, which would sometimes make a movement toward it, but in no case until the small fish had reconnoitered the ground. I worked at him till near dusk, but of no avail, and left

him, concluding that he was not to be cheated. One en-
tire sea bass had been guzzled by the creature, without
value received on my part, and I left him. In conversation with the skipper he said the shark often had a pilot
fish with him, which he had seen. This was news to me,
but as the monster had been pretty well fed, I concluded
I would get a crack at him in the morning. Sure enough,
he was on the spot, and so was I, with tactics changed.
I rigged small gear with my views narrowed down on
small game, and pitched in for the pilot. The first throw
was successful, and as I hauled the little fellow struggling
through the water, the monster made a movement towards him, but he was too clumsy. He evidently wanted
to stay proceedings, but the pilot was on deck, a beautiful silver-sided bright-eyed, zebra-circular, brown-striped
fish, weighing two pounds, an entirely different class of
fish from the shark, his shape much like the perch, but
without teeth, the intimate companion and pilot of a
great 350-pound shark. What a contrast? Daniel Lam-
bert among the Liliputians! A mountain and a mole
hill! But to the shark,—which for the first time began
a new movement, describing a circle around the vessel,
which he followed up through the greater part of the
day. We kept the harpoon in the nettings ready for
use. I was sent to repair a ratline on the fore-topgallant
shrouds, and took a new coil of ratline stuff, and with
the end in my hand made it fast to the back stay, and
one eye on the shark. I noticed he was crossing the
ship's stern and heading so as to rise at her counter. I
slid down by the back stays, capsized the coil of rigging,
made a running bowlin' with the other end, jumped into
the main channels, and as I slipped the bowlin' over his

head, gave it a jam with my right hand, just as the vessel
rolled me on him. My left hand dropped over his nose
and the two forefingers and thumb into the edge of his
mouth. The monster, worse frightened than was your
humble servant, started off abeam as though the evil
one was on his back. Here was a pretty kettle of fish,
while I jumped on deck, caught the line with one hand,
the other dreadfully lacerated, lost my hold and overboard went the whole coil.

The skipper took in the surroundings and sang out,
" Up, there, in the forerigging ! Cut away ! Hurry up,
or we lose our top hamper !" But before the men were
in the rigging the shark fetched up " all standing." The
warp stood the shock and so did the shrouds and back
stay, for the bowlin' had done its duty and the monster
was choked to death. We finally got the bight of the
warp on deck, hauled the game alongside, put the tackle
on, hoisted him on deck, and in the last throe of death,
his expiring effort, he knocked with his tail the cook's
soak barrel all in flitters. We cut off his head, took out
a part of his liver and consigned the carcase to his native
element. After cleaning his jaws he displayed four rows
of splendid teeth, and any man on board could slip it
over his head resting on his shoulders. Now for the
boy, or, as Sam would say, " dis child." He was dancing
about deck in much pain, two fingers and thumb raked
between those rows of teeth, without much flesh on, too
proud to cry and too mad to talk, consoling himself in
all his pain with the idea that he had cheated the shark
and his pilot to death. The marks are now visible on
left hand, and will be useful as I continue to " spin yarns "
and tell the young folks " shark stories." And if at this

late day I exult over this wonderful feat, it is my privilege. Who but this boy would have passed by a good harpoon and take a running bowlin' to put over a shark's nose? Please "show me the man." Piscatorially I can amuse my readers by enumerating some lively scenes, and if I have room at the close of this book, and they will promise to accept it in my language, without fiction or flourishes, they shall have it. I have had the experience. Yes, I have.

But the calm continued, notwithstanding everyone was whistling for a breeze, but to no purpose. It was hot and calm and we could not dodge it. Several large green turtle were seen soundly asleep, but the shark frolic of the day before reminded the skipper that we had been sufficiently excited for the two days and he was not disposed to lower the small boat; so he modestly said, "This calm will last till we get out of it by the drift; we will attend to the turtle some other time, and besides, the sun at meridian is the best time to cheat them." Sam sat in the galley door, his day's duty closed, and his "belly full," a pattern of peace and jollity, in that frame of mind that no doubt "a little child could play wid him in safety." The subject with the old darkey was something to eat, and how to obtain it. "You see dere, boys, dere's alluz dem turtlum in dis lattentude, and de hot sun at noon he comes to de top like a Congo nigger to sun, and da gets drunk wid de heat and falls asleep; den we's jus' scull de boat berry quiet and gingingly alongside, put yuze arms round de fool, heel down de boat and slide he in, jus' like de nigger on de Five Points, when police put he in de lockum up, and he wake up, jus' in time to know he's been fooled. But you jus'

take care dem flippers, da's be jus' like a steamboat.
And den dere's dem stakes, and de stews, and bake and
supes, better dan turkum and oshter sarce.   Oh, dese
Western Islands, some call um 'Zores, better dan any
udder place dis side of Capum Horn for fish and turtlum.
Den you jus' hang he by de hind legs, cut he troat, bleed
he good, cut out de meat, trow um shell overboard, coz
dem hawks-bill turtlum be good for combs; but dese
green turtlum shell be's good for notting."   And the old
negro took down a large carver, run the edge over a hone
and exclaimed, "I'se show you all about it to-morrow,
Buddy, coz de skipper here nose all 'bout dese turtlum,
jus' same as him did 'bout dem sea bass, tudder day,"
and Sam went below for his night's sleep.

The night was quiet, not a brace or sheet had been
started, the vessel with scarcely steerage way on her, and
only occasionally a " cat's paw " from the westward, an
indication that our calm would soon be over; decks
washed down, all hands had breakfast, the jolly boat
taken from her beckets, and now towing astern, all hands
busy at the " spun yarn " mill and an uproarious smoke
issuing from Sam's galley, giving note of his being alive,
and each one with an eye out for turtle; for it was well
understood that we were to try our hand at them.   The
atmosphere was dreadful hot, every breath of wind had
died out, and the craft lost steerage way entirely.   The
skipper and mate with quadrants were in the waist,
ready to catch the sun's meridian, and just as she was
stationary, ready to tip, Mrs. Goodell, one of our lady
missionaries, called the skipper's attention to an object
forty rods off; but his eye was on the sun, and if all the
women in Christendom had asked him a question, it

would have had no response. A few seconds passed, when the old man dropped his quadrant, turned to the mate and said, "She has tipped." The response was in the affirmative, and immediately turning to Mrs. G. he said, "That, Madam, is a green turtle." And in the next breath said to the mate, "Stow away your mill, Mr. Thomas. Boy, haul the boat alongside. Here, Jim Cook, take Joe, man the boat, muffle your oars, board the turtle with the scull oar when within ten rods, and away!"

Now turtle, it is agreed, is not fish, and your humble servant was not particularly interested in this scene. Still, as the *modus operandi* was new, he cast an eye to the boat just as long-spliced Jim was going head first overboard. The turtle was in the boat, but the effort put forth was so great to slide the turtle in, that he lost his balance and exchanged places with the green back; but, like a duck, he was out in an instant, and I remembered Sam's comparison of the flippers to a steamboat. Jim was a great water bird and a mighty pugilist, as you will find, by a scene that occurred at Gibraltar, and in which the boy as usual figured. However, they resumed their oars, came alongside, put the watch tackle on the turtle and landed him on deck, face up. The observed of all observers weighed 125 pounds, when Norwegian Joe, turning to the mate said in his broken English, "He got two two a hind leg, two two a fore leg, and a tail a-most, and a head somewhat like a pincer; now what kind a dom fish you call him, Mr. Mate?" A hearty laugh and the turtle was passed over to Sam for dissection, while the boat was off for more with good success. We scuttled two water casks, put a medium sized turtle in each with a view to keep, put a half dozen on their

backs for future use, let another half-dozen go, filled up
the casks with salt water; had turtle in all forms for
ten days.

The calm still prevailed another day, amid a wonderful
show of turtle, whale, porpoise, dolphin and shark, but
the good skipper, true to his governing principle, refused
to lower a boat or make an effort to obtain any more
plunder. "We have enough," was his reply, and that
was law and gospel. He was an example worthy of imi-
tation by every gentleman piscatorially or turtleisingly
inclined, but he would not object to all hands whistling
up a breeze. Before sundown we discovered quite a little
roll of the sea heaving in from the west and at midnight
took a good spanking breeze and shaped our course for
Cape St. Vincent, bidding adieu to horse latitudes, tur-
tles, sharks and calms,—a glorious relief, a happy exchange. Our passengers seemed to enjoy the trip, having
every comfort and attention possible; never in the way,
and full liberty in all parts of the craft, and were particularly happy with an hour spent with Sam, who, to
cheer them up, always had a cup of coffee or tea, and at
a moment's notice. They were favorites with all the
crew, and made Sam sing "Away down in Dixey" once
a day regular.

We made the cape, having had a beautiful run, and with
a strong current always setting up the straits of Gibraltar,
the wind then east. We worked up to the bay in good
style came to an anchor in ten fathoms of water, making
the run from New York in twenty-five days, eight of
which were passed off the Azores. Our object here was
for mails only. Gibraltar is in lat. 36° 5' N. and long.
5° 22' W. from Greenwich The city lays fronting the

Bay of Algeziras and is a beautiful sight, with a gradual elevation from the bay to near its summit, is heavily fortified on the top, and it affords a prospect of the sea on each side of the rock. The rock is joined to the continent by a low piece of land about half a mile wide, used as a parade ground, and is the only passage to the city by land. The rock is on its north end, joined to this peninsula, and is so near perpendicular that from its port holes excavated in the bluff a person can reach his head out and the soldiers on the parade look like the representatives of Liliputians. The writer with his comrades each took turns in prostrating themselves while the others held us by the heels. We dare not stand up square in the port hole and look down, for even in the mode we adopted it was too frightful to prolong the sight. There are four tiers of port holes, opening into large rooms used for various purposes, and roads leading to them from the city, all excavated in solid rock. The soil is thin and none to be seen except on the west face, where the city lays. History states that the soil was carried there by the Moors. The " King's Armada," or now the Governor's residence, is about the only place for vegetation. This had a beautiful garden of shrubbery and small fruits, with hedges of geranium in great variety. The grounds were full of war material of various kinds. The magazine was also here, and a vast number of heavy guns, and with this wonderful sight the whole air was impregnated with shrubs and flowers.

To stand or sit in this beautiful place, commanding a view of the bay, Algeziras, the strait, Alps Hill on the Barbary side, the city below with the surroundings of horticulture, and the fortifications above you at the sum-

mit, the mind becomes bewildered and the head dizzy.
I can only say that, to be appreciated it must be seen.
The fortifications on the summit are quite extensive and
of immense power, and command the strait, which is
eight miles across. Gibraltar had for years laid the commercial world under tribute, and all vessels bound up
the straits were then compelled to carry a Mediterranean
pass, and the voyage previous the same vessel and skipper were fired into, demanding a show of colors, because
some fool of a lieutenant in command of the fortress
wanted to show a little brief authority. It is a short
story. We were bound into Malaga and beating up the
straits; the wind died out, leaving us above the harbor
of Gibraltar, and a little north of the usual track bound
up, and off the south end of the rock the wind failed us
and we barely had steerage way on the vessel, but from
our position he knew that we were bound to Malaga,
which lays on the main just above the rock. It was
about noon, when bang went a gun, and a shot came
astern of us, at which insult Capt. Storer was considerably disturbed, but he ordered the boy to get the
colors up and waited in hopes the insult would not be
repeated. But he was mistaken, for in two minutes
bang came another shot just ahead. Our skipper knew
the rule, and lest the third shot should be for us, your
humble servant was ordered to run up the stripes and
he did so. But it was a stark calm and they hugged
the mast on a perpendicular. This satisfied the villain
in charge of the fortress, and no more shots were sent.
We went into Malaga, obtained our cargo, and stopped
at Gibraltar for mail, when the authorities claimed five
dollars for each shot; but the plucky little captain re-

4

fused to pay it, telling them to do better if they could. Our readers will remember that long-spliced Jim Cook is one of our mess. Well, Jim was a good sailor, though a great pugilist. I was with him in a previous voyage, and we lay in Gibraltar Bay waiting orders. "Shore liberty" was granted four of us, with a permit from the Governor giving us a wide range for our Sunday stroll. We landed at the "mole" or dock, the only landing by water, a wharf perhaps ten rods wide by fifteen long (a squad of soldiers is its guard), leading through double gates to the city, which is heavily walled. This commanded the only entrance to the city. We landed without hindrance, made a pretty thorough examination of the market place, the Armada, its fortifications, and, being fully warned of the sun-down gun, came down through the gates just as the gun gave the signal to close them, but our boat was not there. The officer in charge very kindly informed us that in ten minutes the mole must be cleared, and if our boat was not on the spot we must take a bumboat, which would cost two dollars. Sailor-like, we had spent the last rial (shilling) on our way down, and the boatman wanted pay in advance. The time was up, we heard the tramp of Johnny Bull's adopted sons, while the sergeant waved his cheese-knife for us to retire. We had but little choice, it was either a wet jacket or a fight, and not a moment to decide before it was "Charge!" "Halt!" giving us still an opportunity to retire. Now Jim was in good fighting trim, and swore he would not move. The next order was "Forward!" and Jim snatched the musket of the left file quick as lightning, and he would have been a dead man if the officer had been disposed, but he cried "Halt!"

and stepped up to Jim, laid his hand on his shoulder and said, with a good-natured smile, "You are made of too good stuff to be shot. Give the man his musket and get into your boat. I like your spunk, and this has saved your life; but remember, if you ever step on this mole and disobey, it will go hard with you." All these scenes passed like the whirl of a breath to us, and we breathed free as we marched to our boat, which had that moment arrived, and the author resolved that rum was not a fit companion for him when on shore in a foreign country, and ever after I chose my associates for shore liberty.

And now for a straight wake. The market place at Gibraltar produces a good display of vegetables, fruit, poultry and fish. It is mostly kept by Jews, Turks and Moors, and is brought over in veluchers or boats from the Barbary side of the straits. The dress of the market men and women is mostly Turkish, quite costly and extravagant. They can all get off a spattering of English. Your humble servant had no difficulty at fourteen years old to market from them without a pilot, provided the "rial" (eight shilling to the dollar) was the basis of the whole finance. Without solicitation my basket was always brought down to the gates by a slave, and if any space was left after filling my list, the little senorita would fill it with grapes and oranges. Whether it was my face or my jaunty chip hat with a long silk ribbon and white duck trowsers without suspenders, that captivated her and her old Jew father, I never knew, but I know that "petit Americano" always met with a grand reception in that market.

Payne says, "The Fortress of Gibraltar was taken 1704 in two days by a combined fleet of English and Dutch ships under command of Sir George Rooke. In the same year, the Spaniards attempted its recapture, at which time it stood out a memorable siege, when 500 of the enemy having scaled the walls on the bay, crept up the rocks during the early morning, were charged upon and driven headlong into the sea, after which it was ceded to the English by treaty in 1713. Spain again made an attempt in 1727 with a powerful army, but raised the siege after laying before it several months. But the blockade and siege it sustained from the same party for nearly four years, from 1779 to 1783, will ever be considered as one of the most remarkable events in history. The combined army of France and Spain, under the Duke de Crillon with 30,000 men attempted to reduce the place by famine and were thrice baffled by relief from England. The last of these succors were thrown in under the command of Lord Howe. By a sally made by him all the outer batteries of the Spaniard were entirely destroyed but with little loss to him. The Spanish monarch adopted a plan to construct ten large floating batteries composed of large timbers of cedar and mahogany, on such a principle as was supposed could not be penetrated by balls. Every arrangement in the power of Spain was made for the capability of pouring destruction on the place in a tremendous manner. On the 13th of September, 1782, the attack was made. The brave and able Governor brought forth every exertion to repel it, and for this purpose prepared an immense number of red hot balls, which were made effectual. The whole Armada took fire, became unmanageable, and almost all the devoted wretches who had embarked in them were totally destroyed by fire and water.* At this siege the Spanish batteries discharged showers of shot and shell, having 400 pieces of the heaviest artillery playing in connection with the water batteries, the whole a grand exhibition of warfare without its parallel in the world. The garrison discharged 80,000 red hot shot during the attack, and when the enemy was totally defeated the generous humanity of the victors was conspicuous in saving the lives of the vanquished enemies even at the hazard of their own." At Algeziras, on the bay, was a stone castle built by O'Hara, who took an oath that he would occupy it until Gibraltar surrendered. It was in good repair in 1821, and was called "O'Hara's folly." Gibraltar Bay is in the form of a horse shoe, and is not very good holding ground for a severe souther.

During a Levanter (gale from east), I have seen three tiers of clouds ranging on the west side over the city, plainly showing the fortifications on the summit, with its flag on the staff above the upper stratum of clouds, a singular object and seemed to be perched up in the heavens without anything to support it. It is one and a fourth miles above the sea. As before stated, the east side of the rock is nearly a perpendicular, and cannot be climbed or rather never has—and in looking at it, approaching from the Atlantic, it somewhat resembles a sperm whale—and viewing it from opposite the strait, the whale is split, the east side thrown away. The tail

---

* This Armada was visible at the bottom of the bay to the author in 1819. It lies in about five fathoms of water, near the mole. The whole bay is white sand, and in ten fathoms of water we sighted our anchors every day to see if they were foul.

is the most southern point in Europe.   Our mail obtained,
a little marketing done at the old Jew stall, and a very
pretty "adieu, Senore Americano," from the little Jew-
ess, and, loaded down with fruit, we got under way for
Malta.   Had a splendid run to Mount Stromboli, an
uninhabited burning mountain making up from the sea,
in the form of a sugar loaf.   Its south end is a bold
shore, while a reef extends a long distance on its north
end.   We passed it southerly, the main current setting
east; the wind left us when about three miles off, and
unfortunately in the eddy which set directly on it.   I
compare the island with Faulkner's Island, in Long Isl-
and Sound, excepting that Stromboli is mountainous, its
crater on the top.   The weather was fine.   The dog
watch was set, not a breath of wind.   The skipper cast
his eye at the barometer, and ordered, "Lower down
both top-gallant-sails, man your clue lines, let go your
sheets, and send down both yards.   Come, hurry there,
men—hurry up, Mr. Thomas," and the men were stretch-
ing their necks to learn the cause, but the skipper did
not see fit to enlighten any body but the mate.   It was
just seventeen minutes, and the yards were on deck.
The skipper immediately ordered, "close-reefed top-sails,
jib furled, and spanker double-buttoned—the fore and
main courses furled snug," and in twenty minutes more
the little brig was snug as a bug.   The eddy tide had
set toward the north point and swept us not more than a
mile off the island.   Everything about decks was well
secured, her head had been placed to southward; port
tacks aboard, when in an instant the Levanter was on
us, the lee-rail under.   The skipper had the last sight of
the island, and it was now as dark as pitch, but in that

last bearings he figured that by "keel-hauling" occasionally she would just "rub and go,"—not a thing but the foam about the vessel to be seen. Mr. Thomas was on the windlass-bits. I carried the message, "Can you see the surf? If so, tell me how it bears?" "Nothing yet, sir," and the skipper gave her a squeeze of two points. She shot up into the wind and off again, and thus he played her, but it seemed as if her masts would jump out of her. The anxiety about decks was immense, for if she struck it was certain death. "Land, O," was the next message to the skipper. It blew so that he could only hear with one ear to leeward. "Do you see the land, or the clear water beyond? If so, how does it bear?" was the message, and again I went back with: "Two points under the lee bow, surf!" and again: "Three points," when the skipper gave her another squeeze, and off again instantly, but she quivered, and the next: "Surf, four points," and again: "Open sea, abeam," and again: "Open sea, abaft the beam," and Captain Peter stuck his head under the spanker-boom, saw he was going clear, sent for the mate, and said: "Thank God, she is safe, come aft; we will put her head to northward, and lay her under the storm staysail." Here was a relief, though it was "rub and go," and done by close calculation, and previous preparation. If the barometer had not been consulted, or the skipper had not heeded her indications, nothing could have saved us, for there was no room to wear ship, and she never could have stayed under short sail, and further, if he had made no preparation before the Levanter was on, she would have been on a lee shore before sail could have been shortened. "Coming events, with him, cast shadows before," and he was always on the lookout for them. Who but my old schoolmaster, would think of placing a ship in trim for a gale, when a calm and clear sky prevailed? But what were the indications? I answer, a roll of the sea from the east; falling of the barometer, and in the season of Levanters.

Now it gives the author much real satisfaction to place the honors on the good, kind-hearted old salt, and I propose to hurry forward this little narrative, in order that before his voyage of life is closed, he shall have the knowledge of my sincere and earnest thanks, publicly expressed, for his kindness to me in the days that are past. It is my earnest wish that he may have a pleasant closing up of life, a triumphant death, and a harbor in Christ's kingdom, where he will need no chart, compass, or barometer, and where the sea of glory will not be disturbed with Strombolis or Levanters. But to resume.

The gale held us about eighteen hours. Wind hauled to northward; laid our course again for Malta; passed Stromboli with a good berth, and sighted the island in three days; it lays in lat. 35° 54' N., long. 14° 28' E. from Greenwich. We were signaled when about eight miles off, and soon surrounded with boats, all clamorous for the job of towing. Finally, as it was calm, a bargain was made for two strings, twenty-four boats, and away we went four knots an hour, and anchored in a beautiful harbor, completely land-locked, and in ten fathoms of water. This harbor was for fishermen and quarantine. In the center of the harbor is a small island with fortifications and the lazaretto. The island lies about sixty miles south of Sicily—is twenty miles long and twelve wide, containing five beautiful harbors, with all necessary fortifications, and all safe anchorages. The main commercial city is called Valetta. At the foot of this harbor is the English Navy Yard. In 1785 the whole population of the island was 150,000. The entrance to Valetta harbor is about half a mile in width, and continues that width for considerable distance, then opening into a beautiful bay, extending two miles from the sea, and is immensely fortified on each point of entrance. In 1821, as the writer entered this harbor, there was on the left side four gibbets or gallows, on each of which was hanging in a swivel chain a human body, two containing skeletons, one with considerable flesh on it, one still alive, and hundreds of turkey buzzards feeding on the carcases. The scene was awful beyond description. On inquiry ashore, we found that all persons found guilty of piracy were condemned to this horrid mode of death. The one alive was encased the day before, having been condemned as a Moorish pirate. The rock of this whole island is a cream color, quite soft, and easily excavated. Large reservoirs are made for the deposit of wheat and provisions, and in early days sufficient for five years' supply was kept there. The language is Arabic and Italian, with but little English. Valetta is the great thoroughfare for the eastern world, and the key for Asia and Africa. Craft of almost every nation and rig are here to be found. The people are well educated in European customs, and though extravagant in dress, are courteous in the extreme to strangers. The city is supplied with water, led from near the ancient city of " Milite," through masonry supported by 1,000 arches, and is distributed through the Marina with occasional fountains free to all. This Marina or dock fronting the city, is the great promenade on Sunday, which is their best day of recreation. The weather is extremely hot in the city, but the Marina with its occasional shade and breeze, makes it a charming place. Fruit and wine are good, plenty and cheap. The city abounds in churches, the largest of which is St. Paul's, which in company with the Mate I gave a thorough examination in 1820. It is massive in size, quite ancient in architecture, built with native stone, and beautifully polished outside and in, a vestibule opening into the body of the church, unobstructed by seats or partition, except an altar inclosed in heavy railings of solid silver, confession boxes on castors, six on each side. The whole floor mosaic of various colors in marble, representing the cross, various saints, battle scenes, our Saviour, and many others; the work so finely done that no unevenness or roughness could be felt, and was a dazzling sight as we viewed it from the entrance. When Napoleon in his raid for plunder in Italy, sacked this island, the costly railing round the altar of this church escaped the notice of the plunderers, by reason of its heavy coat of lead paint, which had never been extracted, except in occasional places, by " wear and tear,"—though the rascally thieves took all the ornaments of gold and silver hanging on the walls they could find, said by our worthy sexton, " to amount to over 100,000 pasos" (dollars). However, the walls must have recuperated in the same line of goods, for they were full,—offerings made to the saints, in silver and gold, for favors granted or petitioned for. The egress and ingress of people was immense. The confession boxes drove a thriving trade—the whole, without confusion or noise, every person stepping lightly and in soft slippers, two pairs being furnished myself and comrade by the sexton, who could prate a little poor English. I may as well here say that our sexton having on our arrival received a bright Mexican dollar, was quite disposed to show all that was to be seen within his jurisdiction, and after being satisfied with the sights on the first floor, lighted each a wax candle, and led the way to the basement,—assuring us that this was the embalmed body of "St. Paul," this was "St. Peter," that was the "Virgin Mary," and by the number of bodies before us, he would have gone through the whole catalogue of saints, popes, and cardinals, had not I said to my companion " this spatters too much of the marvellous for me. It savors of catacombs; let us get fresh air." So we abruptly put a stop to the proceedings, and turned towards the stairs, crying, " Muche marlo, Signor." " No caress." " Nente boano, Signor." And we passed up and out, exchanging slippers while the sexton pointed us to the font of holy water in the vestibule, and to please him we both took a tip.

But let us say a word about the north harbor. Our captain reported to our consignee, through the Custom House at the lazaret, a small building with iron railing leading to low water mark, within the enclosure where all boats during the quarantine of their vessels must communicate on a platform with folding doors opening into a large room, and a soldier on guard to prevent further intrusion. A pole of fifteen feet is run out with a slit in the end to receive your communications without the touch; it is then cut through and through by stamp, held over a smoke, and in that state presented to the officers of Customs. No communication can be received

any other way, and thus our skipper communicated with
his consignee at Valetti, and entered his vessel. They
met next day by appointment, talked between the bars,
passed papers and letters through the smoke, obtained
protigue to land our passengers in two days after being
examined in person at the old smoke house, and liberty
to take the vessel to town in five days; provided the
examination of passengers was satisfactory, and also that
he should produce officers, crew and passengers every
morning at 8 o'clock at the "Lazarett." We took all
hands to the great smoke house, were scrutinized closely,
made to jump twice, and without the chop block, or the
aid of smoke, all was satisfactory, and during all this
humbuggery, we were kept twenty feet from the officers.
The whole operation, childish and uncivil, a disgrace to
the Island of Malta and the English flag. Next morning we took all hands ashore, formed a line on a platform, skipper at the head and Sam at the rear—an exhibition of the two extremes of beauty. Messrs. Goodell
and Bird, with their wives, were beautiful and noble,
while Sam, though gloriously good, was the most awk-
ward, ill-looking piece of humanity on the continent, all
except his eyes. When it came Sam's turn to jump, he
substituted the song and dance of "Away down in
Dixey," to the great amusement of officers and soldiers.
The door of the great "Sanhedrim" closed amid three
rousing cheers with a tiger, and gave its echo through
the bay and city, to the wonder and astonishment of the
people. At the time appointed, our passengers were
received at the Lazarett by their friends, intending to
remain at Valetti previous to their departure for Jerusalem, by way of Joppa. Thus were they safely landed

after a confinement in small dimensions during forty-seven days, beloved by every soul on board the vessel, fit messengers to spread glad tidings of great joy through the plains and mountains of Palestine.

Agreeable to decree we obtained *protique* and shifted anchorage to Valetti. The following Sunday, with the mate, having obtained a permit from the Governor with full range of the island, we took a carriage, much after the Cuban style, to see the ancient city of Melite, where Paul was shipwrecked, and to examine St. Paul's cave, both about ten miles distant by land. The road led through a country of the "vine and fig tree," fruit of their season plenty and cheap, grapes and bread the staple. Advice from friends induced us to convert two Spanish dollars into the small fractional of their currency for the miserable Ladrone by whom we should be infested, and it proved a judicious movement. We reached the entrance to the cave, fortunately found the soldier and guide at their post, to whom we tendered the examination of our permit, and before it was read by the soldier we were beset by about 500 men, women and children, the most miserable, filthy beggars, half-starved, clamorous, more like wolves than human, the offscouring of the old dilapidated city. We were prepared to see beggars, owls and satyrs, but not such a crew. We had the antidote, however, and threw broadcast a handful of change. The iron gate was open and we crowded in, but each of us minus a handkerchief and glad to get off at that. We entered the cave with the guide, the soldier outside of but little use to us; his sympathies were with the Ladrone, not us. We entered the cave

with candles, the guide and my right-hand supporter in
my pocket, and during this subterranean passage I chose
to be in the rear. The atmosphere was not depressing,
nor the passages small. We opened into large, square
rooms connected with passages and similar rooms, all
cut through the rock, but of various sizes. We followed
the first one perhaps half a mile, observing that new passages led off in other directions. They were all uniform
in size, eight feet high and five feet wide, rooms about
eighteen feet square, of equal height as the passages,
which were circuitous. The ceilings, walls and floors
smooth, apparently done by square and level. We entered the cave facing about south. The rooms and passages above described were on our left hand. At the
right on entering were two similar rooms connecting
with two smaller, evidently for cooking purposes, though
I saw no outlet for smoke. One of these rooms had
niches cut, some upright and others horizontal, apparently for the dead, or as a substitute for bedsteads.
They were of different sizes, from the adult to the infant.
The whole interior of these various excavations we judged
covered a space of ten acres. Our guide insisted that the
first passage named extended to near the new city, and
another continued westerly to near the sea, and that if
we would give ourselves time, take a foot guide, in a day
we could see the road as it left the cave and afterwards
trace it to its termination at the sea. To corroborate
this, Payne quotes Brydone thus: "That on this side of
the island are still vestiges of several ancient roads,
with tracks worn deep in the rocks. These roads are
now terminated by the precipice with the sea beneath,
and shows that the island has in former ages been of

larger size than at present, but the convulsion that occasioned its diminution is probably much beyond the reach of any history or tradition."

The cave is certainly a wonderful production, and to give a full and thorough description of it needs more time than two sailor boys can give. Our guide was an Englishman, well educated, and was fully conversant with the winding passages of this cave. It is an immense excavation, and the writer hazards the opinion that a stranger without a compass placed twenty rods within it, minus a guide, would starve before he could find his way out. We spent two hours in constant movement and knew but little about the cave. This, said our guide, was done by St. Paul and his followers after he was cast away, and pointing, as we came to the light of day to a little inlet not rifle shot off, said, "there is where he landed under pressure of a "Levanter." No rubbish or moisture was seen or felt in the cave, and the atmosphere as easy to breathe as if outside.

Now the author is inclined to believe that poor Paul never had anything to do with that kind of business. In my opinion his time was fully occupied in preaching the Gospel. He had too much courage to dig an asylum underground, and Jonah-like, flee from duty to save his life. It was not in him to crawl into a cave, and beside, all the disciples with all their friends could not build that cave in two centuries. Listen to history: "The Phocians were the original occupants of Malta and were driven out by the Phœnicians; these by the Greeks; and passed from them to the Carthagenians; from them to the Romans; who were subdued by the Goths; then by the Saracens; from whom in 1090 the Normans;

after which it had the same masters as Sicily, till Charles
V. gave it to the Knights of Malta and Jerusalem."
In those days to the victor came the spoils. A part of
the spoils were whole towns and cities made prisoners
from Asia and Africa and used as slaves. The millions
of poor that could not pay a ransom were like cattle,
sent to different parts to labor, and half starved to die.
No doubt these plunderers sent some of those slaves to
Malta to labor and to death. Paul's was a mission of
peace, not of war. He did not fight for gold, territory,
or prisoners. What, think you, became of millions upon
millions of slaves or prisoners taken by Alexander,
Darius, Cyrus, Hannibal, the Carthagenians, Rome, and
even Napoleon, during their raids for gold and plunder
in this same country of which we write, and if you get
no satisfactory reply, come back to a more recent date
and consult the Knights of Malta and Jerusalem, and
you will say with me that Paul dug no caves, but these
powerful and aristocratic knights did. These men evidently wielded an immense power, and any Sir Knight
holding a gavel could, by the stroke of a pen at five
days' notice send 50,000 prisoners to Malta to dig this
cave, to which the order itself could flee when they in
their turn should be overwhelmed. Let the reader understand that the Knights of Malta and Jerusalem were
not akin to the Templars of our day, but as opposite as
day is to night; the former seeking power and plunder,
aristocratic, not valuing human life as a feather; the
latter, Samaritans, good, kind, protectors of human life,
governed by the principles of faith, hope and charity.

We left the cave in full belief that Paul never darkened its portals, and as in the case of the bodies of the

saints mouldering in the deep, dark basement of Saint
Paul's Church, before described. We took no stock in
what our guide said. Legend and tradition, much like
old fogy's gossip, "grows with age and opportunity,"
and yet this does not affect the magnitude of this whole
enterprise. We gave the guide his dollar, and following
his directions were soon on the spot where the "anointed
of God" was shipwrecked. It lies in front of the old
city, on a bold, rocky shore on a small inlet, and an iron
shaft on a large boulder rock, the surroundings answering
the Bible history, and we had no doubt it was the iden-
tical spot where the "two seas met."

Our next move was for a stroll among the ruins of
Melite, a wonderful sight, and at the first view of this
ruined city, once containing 150,000 inhabitants, I exclaimed, Good God! from whence proceed such melancholy revolutions? Why are so many cities destroyed?
Why is not that ancient population reproduced and per-
petuated? The temples are thrown down, the palaces
demolished, the ports filled up. The town is destroyed
and stripped of all good inhabitants, and the beggar and
the outcast only are left. It seems a dreary burying place.
This ancient city is a mass of ruins, peopled by beggars
and fishermen, "who dry their nets on the rocks." The
ruins found here, prove that it was once the abode of
luxury and opulence, but "baldness has come upon it."
"It is forsaken and bereaved of its king. The owl and
the raven (Turkey buzzard) dwell therein. The mirth
and the harp ceaseth, the joy of the tabret also cease.
They that dwell therein are desolate. The stranger that
shall come from a far land shall say, 'I will give the city
into the hand of strangers for a prey, for the robbers

5

shall enter into it and defile it.'" And with these prophecies in my mind, associated with the cave in question, I
said, Can it be that this is the judgment on this people
for murdering by inches, in starvation and disease, millions upon millions of poor innocent prisoners taken from
the interior of Asia and Africa, and doomed to labor at
Melite for the gratification of a few men, before enum-
erated, who roamed over this beautiful country for con-
quest and gold? Is this the fulfillment of prophecies
applicable to this place? This is not Babylon, and yet
it is a part of "the country of the Jews." It is Palestine, "one of the isles of the sea." I turned my back
on the scene and again mingled in civilization, for we
had witnessed naught but desolation and misery. We
gave another broadcast throw of small coin among the
crowd of beggars that had covered our rear since we
emerged from the cave, jumped into our calash, unlocked
a private apartment in the carriage, drew forth our bottle
of splendid Catania wine, eight pounds of grapes, a loaf
of bread, and "talked by the way" home. On the following Sunday, at the quarters of the American consul,
we attended religious services with our missionaries,
shook hands with all, wished them a safe trip to Joppa,
and parted. We heard from them at Jerusalem on the
twelfth day after. We discharged part of our cargo,
and during our stay were overwhelmed with beautiful
fruit in great variety at small cost, offered us by bum-
boats.

My last trip on shore, if not profitable was certainly
eventful, and your humble servant the hero. A lighter
load of dye woods had been landed on the Marina, the
boy left in charge till the carman came. I mounted the

pile, pockets full of grapes, and a hickory stick in my hand. I soon found that dock wallopers abounded here as well as in New York, and equally as bold; for, without much ceremony, three loafers pitched in for plunder, and without any less ceremony I brought them to with the hickory, one with a broken finger, and drove them off. They soon brought reinforcements, and about a dozen of the whelps surrounded the pile. This drew quite a concourse of people, and they claimed I should have a fair shake. My position was again on top of the pile, when the largest loafer took up a stick as bold as a lion; but, before he got outside the circle, he was floored with the full force of the stick across his shoulders, and as I turned to assume my former position two others pitched in to avenge their comrade and I got a peeler across the nose and lost half my shirt. The crowd had by this time been augmented to about 500 people. One of my antagonists was outside with a broken arm, but I mounted, and as I did so I noticed a soldier on the trot coming one way, and old Sam with an oar in his hand from the other, the latter yelling, "I'se cummin' Massa Charley!" and before he got through the crowd a chap opened his dirty shirt bosom and threw a louse at me. Now it did not make any difference with me whether it was a reality or a sham. I made for him and fetched him also. We were in the tussle when Sam's voice was over me, "Hold on, Massa Charley! hold on, I'se here!" And he cut a swath on one end of the mob, while the soldier cleared the way on the other, and amid the cheers of the people we both started for the boat, assisted by the soldier, who, having had the rights of the thing explained, escorted us both to the boat and took the three

wounded loafers to the guard house.   The carman had
arrived, took possession of the wood and we came aboard.
You may depend, I was covered with blood and quite a
dirty looking subject.   The morning's Gazette reported
the " Yankee boy " as having whipped out three loafers
who attempted to steal from him.   One a finger broken,
one an arm ditto, and the other considerably bruised, all
committed to the guard house.   I could not afford
another fight lest my blows would not be as lucky in my
defense and kept the ship, though crowds of the dirty
creatures were on the Marina every day, waiting a chance.
My only fear in the meleé was the stiletto.

Having all in readiness, we got under way for Messina,
in Sicily, about sixty miles distant.   The second day we
made the island, having had moderate winds, and by nine
o'clock P. M. becalmed in the strait and abreast of Mount
Ætna, and two miles from shore.   The crater was in
action, throwing out upon the water and surroundings
a frightful red glare.   The famous whirlpools of Charybdis
were outside of us, not more than two miles, and a stark
calm.   The position was anything but pleasant, no
anchorage, and a strong current setting through the
strait, and it made a long, gloomy night, not a star or
speck of land to be seen.   The elevation of the light,
alternated by smoke and fire, thrown on us from sudden
flashes, was a scene beyond my ability to describe.   Immense quantities of lava flowed down the mountain, and
the surface of the water in the morning was covered with
pummice.   It is generally admitted that a sympathy exists
between Ætna and Stromboli, never burning together.
The latter was inactive as we passed it going up, and the
former had ceased to burn on our passage down, but we

found Stromboli in full blast. I propose to give a pretty thorough description of Ætna by reason of a personal inspection I gave it while lying at Messina.

While we lay at Messina, Ætna gave evidence of her internal troubles by three shocks of sufficient magnitude to frighten the inhabitants to seek protection on the Marina. It was estimated that 20,000 people rushed there and gathered in clusters around a priest, each clinging to another, touching, if possible, the hem of his garment, and I noticed that the same virtue was expected from a young priest of twelve as of an aged friar. The dress is alike in black, and all wear a chapeau in the same manner that the captain of the New Haven Artillery wore as a part of his regimentals in 1812, vide Egbert P——. Ætna did not repeat her throb, and the people at sundown went home. We entered the harbor of Messina in the morning, doomed to five days quarantine, where every morning all hands were formed in line, fronting the health officers, and (as at Malta) obliged to jump up and down twice at least, and in regular order of grade, but privileged to dance as a substitute. Before we obtained *pratique* there was so much anxiety to see our old cook dance that it was understood the services should commence with our crew first. This would enable all concerned to be present on that momentous occasion, in which Sam's dance and song of "Away down in Dixey" was the governing feature, for he could sing as well as dance it. In due time we hauled over to the city across the bay, and of course had liberty of the city. The Marina is about two miles long, of rectangular form, fronting the city, divided by a strong wall, is wide, beautiful and commodious, and one of the finest walks

in the city.   A portion of it is shaded with trees, a front
view of the shipping, the forts, and the bay.   Nearly all
nations are represented here, and on Sunday the ships are
dressed out in bunting.   Like Malta, Sunday is the holi-
day and is devoted to amusement.   It is no uncommon
thing to see 15,000 people on the promenade.   Water
fountains are in profusion; fruit and lemonade pedlers
also.   Various fountains, representing Hercules, Neptune,
and various knights, and animals, each with several jets
of water leading into reservoirs, free to all.   The police
department is quite effective.   The Marina is swept clean
by the chain-gang every morning by sunrise.   The writer,
in all his stay in Sicily, never saw a native the worse
for liquor.   That habit was only embraced by foreigners,
with a wonderful ascendancy in favor of the English and
Yankees.

The island produced fine beef and mutton, with a
world of nuts, oranges and figs.   The climate is so hot
that even in our winter the shade is refreshing.   Chilly
winds in the day are only felt in March.   The only
appearance of winter is found near the summit of Ætna,
where snow is sometimes seen.   And now for Mount
Ætna.   Figures I have borrowed from Brydone, who
like myself visited this wonderful curiosity.   In making
the island of Sicily it looks like an immense chimney.
The ascent to the crater by way of Catanea is said to
be 30,000 paces, but by Roudazzo is only 20,000.
Ætna is divided into three distinct regions; these three
are as different, both in climate and productions, as the
three zones of the earth, and may be styled with propri-
ety, the torrid, the temperate, and the frigid zones.
The first region surrounds the foot of the mountain, and

forms the most fertile country in the earth on all sides of it, to the height of about fifteen miles; where the woody region begins, it is composed almost entirely of lava, which after many ages is at length converted into the most fertile soil. The woody region, or temperate zone, is composed of one vast forest that extends all around the mountain. Here are enormous chestnut trees, one of which, "castagno de cento cavilli," which for some centuries past has been looked upon as one of the greatest wonders of Ætna. The appearance is like that of five trees growing together, but Recupero has found that all the stems unite under ground in one root, and on close examination, it is discovered that these five trees were once really united in one. There is a large opening in the middle measuring 204 feet around, that was once occupied by solid timber.

The circumference of the temperate zone is not less than seventy miles. The barren region, or frigid zone, is marked by a circle of snow and ice, which extends on all sides to the distance of about eight miles. In the center of this circle the great crater of the mountain rears its burning head, and the region of intense cold and of intense heat seems to be forever united in the same point. This last region the writer calls the fourth region, or that of fire, which has given being to all the rest. The crater is a circle of about three and a half miles in circumference, and forms a hollow like a vast amphitheater, and is so hot that it is dangerous and unsafe to enter it. Still it has been done by several parties; once by Commodore Elisha Peck, U. S. Navy, formerly a resident in New Haven, Conn., but now dead. He said he put a silver dollar in the slit of a long pole

and dipped it in the liquid lava. The author was fully
satisfied with feasting his eyes on this wonderful sight,
and had no desire to step over the edge of the crater,
even when the mountain was quiet. It is still very generally supposed by these Sicilians, that Ætna is the
mouth of hell, and that Anna Boleyn has been burning
in the mountain during two centuries, for the crime of
inducing Henry VIII. to renounce the religion of the
Church of Rome. Thucydides is the most early writer
who speaks of eruptions from Ætna, and enumerates
three at the close of his book; the latter of these hap-
pened in the spring 424 B. C., and another fifty years
earlier, but to the first he gives no date. Pindar
composed an ode in the 78th Olympiad, five years after
the second eruption mentioned by Thucydides, in which
he describes that scene, and retains the ridiculous notion
held by the ancients, that Jupiter had buried many
giants under Mount Ætna, and their struggling to get
loose was the cause of its eruptions. Eucretus has
spoken of the cause which produced the eruption in his
6th book. In the year 1669 a violent eruption continued
six weeks, and the lava in its course overwhelmed fourteen towns and villages, destroying 3,000 inhabitants.
Twelve years after, the city of Catanea was entirely
overwhelmed by a tremendous earthquake, felt through
Sicily, Malta, and the Continent, by which 93,000 people suffered death. Since that time there have been
three remarkable eruptions—in 1753, 1755, and 1783.
In the latter year the lava reached Palermo, and caused
great destruction in its course. Since that time it has had
twelve slight eruptions. The inhabitants of Sicily are a
social, sprightly people, quite extravagant in dress, and

use Sunday for promenade and amusements. The Marina is the great place of attraction, in which sailors from the shipping usually mingle to a large extent. Numbers of jacks or "borckas" are brought on the ground to hire to the sailors to ride; price one dollar a day. They are a small animal, long ears, and make quite an interesting whinny, especially in the excitement usual on such occasions. Their gait is a kind of shuffling pace, and are sometimes quite fast. They are better suited for packing than the saddle, but in the absence of horses, are well adapted for sailors. Our crew ·voted a "borcka" ride, and with old Sam, of course, we walked ashore one Sunday morning, having previously ordered six of those interesting locomotives. Old Sam was always counted in, on all occasions of frolic; in fact he was a necessity, for we generally went Scott free when he was with us. His pleasant, funny face, and frolicsome gestures, mixed with music and dancing, commanded respect, together with all the fruit and wine we wanted. The jacks arrived in front of our vessel, and on this extraordinary occasion it brought a great crowd. A jack was reserved for Sam, that had been educated to balk unless punched with a sharp instrument forward of the saddle; the secret was with the mulcteer and myself. We mounted amid the cheers of 2,000 people, but the darkey was the center of attraction, with his Sunday toggery, looking (all but color) like a midshipman, his face radiant with smiles, whip and umbrella in hand, mounted, or, I should more properly say, straddled the jack, both feet reaching the ground, gathered up the reins and sang out, "Go lang, horse, go lang smoonly," pressed him with his knees, and to his astonishment the jack braced his fore feet and would not move a hair's breadth, but opened his mouth with a whinny of extraordinary length and power, which was answered by his fellows all over the Marina, but he would not go. We turned back to see the sport, amid an uproar of cheers from the crowd. It was a rich scene. Sam stood facing the jack, talking Congo, Italian and English amalgamated, addressed to the animal in tones of endearment so soft and smooth that anything but a jack would have softened into compliance; patted him, rubbed down his short legs, sent on board for a biscuit, took up his fore feet, and finally, a little out of patience, took up both hind legs, wheelbarrow-fashion, but it was no go. The jack was a fixture. The crowd increased in numbers as the scene grew interesting, but finally the muleteer put in his appearance, saw that Sam was well straddled, handed him the reins, whispered in the jack's ear, gave the punch, and away he went, heels in the air, Sam with a good hug round the animal's neck, but the rider kept his position; the animal quieted down and covered the rear of our cavalcade. With his blue umbrella, Sam rode as proudly as a king, having a care that his black face should not be made the whiter by reason of the sun. We returned into the Marina about 3 o'clock, with an immense crowd in our wake, "order of march reversed;" Sam on the right, and well did he deserve the honors, the waving of handkerchiefs from the dwellings, and the cheers from the streets. He returned the salutes by a tip of that laced cap as graceful as any of our newly-elected governors at their inauguration, and it would astonish any of our white officials. I well remember the beautiful Grecian bend of that long neck, the white teeth, and those long legs operating as propellers to a velocipede. The whole thing a grand ovation from beginning to end. We were loaded down with choice cakes, flowers, and fruits, and I doubt if Earl Roger in 1130, as he passed over the same ground, on his return from the Holy Land, received more attention than the jolly crew of the Shepherdess did in 1822— and wonderful to relate, we were all sober, and not an insult was offered us during the day. Good for the people of Messina!

Our return cargo was wine, oranges, lemons, and bird seed, and we bid adieu to Sicily, bound for New York. Passed Stromboli on the third, and Gibraltar on the eighth day out. Came through the strait in company with eighty sail of vessels. Our readers may remember the calm we endured in the horse latitude, on our outward passage. We were now reaping the harvest of that eight days spent among the fish. The vessel's bottom was completely covered with clam barnacles, to that extent that seven knots an hour was the best speed, with a favorable breeze, and they were growing fast. Various experiments were tried to extract them, one of which was to sling the boy in a bolin' over the vessel's counter with a hoe, but it was of no use. We had the Atlantic to cross, with a portion of cargo perishable, and in view of this our skipper was uneasy in the extreme, and barnacles of the clam species grew fast. The only consolation was, we could count on good fishing during the passage. About midway across we took a severe gale, with a heavy cross-sea, wind about west. We got the vessel in good trim and hove her to. Grog was ordered by the skipper, and to save the old cook the job, I took the tin pot to the cabin, crawled out of door, waited for a good chance to dodge the seas, and made a dive for the lee of the long boat. Sam had kept his eye on the boy, and lest he should get washed overboard, he stepped out of the galley at the time I was reaching for the boat's gripe, and at the instant a tremendous sea broke all over the decks and boat, which lifted me off my feet, lost my hold, and as the vessel surged to windward, I was going over the lee rail head first in the receding sea, but the watchful old cook jumped into the waste, grabbed my heel, and hauled me on deck—tin pot in left hand, but rum all gone—and with his eyes full of water, shoved me up to the galley, got a good hold, and tried to speak; he finally succeeded, with that sweet smile, even under the excitement, and said: "Massa Charley, we're safe agin'; but child, done you get de grog no more for de men; we'll jus lef 'um get dare owns grog, but we're safe; now tank God for dat;" and he clapped both arms around me like the hug of a great bear, and cried like a child for joy; and after throwing off the water from my stomach, I was in pretty good condition, made better by a pot of good coffee and a slapper. Fresh water flowed freely from Sam's eyes, where a few moments before he was blinded with salt. True affection and reciprocal on my part, for when Sam let go his hold to save your hum-. ble servant, his chance for life was but little better than mine, but he did not count the cost. The gale continued to increase, and hauled more southerly, with a tremend-ous chop, and unsafe to scud. During the night the wind veered westerly, and it seemed as if the little craft could not weather it, at times the sea boarding her from opposite directions at the same time, but like the duck, she would shake herself, ready for another wallow. "Waist boards" were all out. Forecastle hatch battened down, dead lights in, and the vessel again under the storm stay-sail. This was all we could do for her, whether she went up or down, and, sailor-like, we were disposed to accept the circumstances, certainly a happy frame of mind to be in. She worried all night at it; seemed to be in good heart in the morning, when the wind died out, and we made sail. On an examination of my log, I find that in the year previous we took a gale of greater magnitude in the same latitude and craft, under charge of same skipper, and if the reader will bear with me I will relate it.

We were bound home from Malaga, deeply loaded with raisins, in which your humble servant was one of the crew. The gale was from the west. Put the vessel under short sail, sent down topgallant yards and hove her to. The sea and gale increasing, we took in everything, and set the old favorite "storm stay-sail," on the main stays, its hoist on the mainmast. Tack on an iron strap on the foremast over the cook's galley, and sheets hauled aft, containing but thirty yards heavy canvass, and during twelve hours she made good weather, until the wind canted up good N. N. E., and increased to a tornado. The crew were taken out of the forecastle, hatches well secured, dead lights all in, life lines run outside the rail between the standing rigging, decks all clear, waist-boards out, and at meridian the gale still increased. Our Mate, Mr. Isaac English, was below, sick, your humble servant installed second Mate *ad interim*. We all stood at the break of the quarter-deck. The skipper as calm as a clock, his eye to windward, and aloft, and the sea, by reason of the great force of the wind, was smooth, apparently one mass of foam, rushing and hissing, and with it in mighty power came the puff, it struck the vessel; she yielded to its force, and in an instant was on her beam ends, an unwieldy mass of wood and iron. This required immediate action, for if she lay in this position till the return of the sea (which was sure to follow) she would never rise again. The wind was fearful as the requiem sounded through the blocks and rigging, and the little brig could not respond. She was, while in that position, dead, and bid fair to be our coffin. The skipper turned to his best man and yelled in his ear: "Go forward, cut the stay-sail becket, and let it go up." The man hesitated; he turned to another, and he refused—coward, as he was; when, understanding the situation, I pulled off my cap and coat, and started, but the skipper's hand was on my shoulder, and putting his mouth to my ear, said: "No, boy, I want you here. If I get washed overboard, you must get her before the wind, but don't cut away the rigging, the sea will be on again when the wind lulls; if I succeed, right your helm when she gets way on her," and cat-like he mounted over on her side, caught hold of the life-line, lost his footing twice before he reached the fore rigging, crawled round to the "cat heads," to the "stay-sail nettings," out knife and cut—up went the "stay-sail" like a shot from a gun, took the wind, she paid off beautifully, gradually gathered way, and like a bird came up on her keel, with life. I saw Captain Peter as she righted, making fast the stay-sail halyards, up to his neck in water, and with his right hand giving motion for three cheers, though I doubt that he heard them himself. As she came on to her keel the boy met her with her helm, and off she went a living, breathing thing. The Captain came aft, without any visible excitement, got the yards square, and as he stepped on to the quarter-deck, with a look of withering scorn, in a loud voice, said: "Try the pumps, you cowards; and go below till I call you!" Agreeably to his prophecy, the sea, as though having gained new energies, rolled and threshed worse than ever. We took in the storm stay-sail, set the close-reefed main top-sail, and the good man with the boy "scud" her "trick a trick" till the gale abated.

"Honor to whom honor is due." He was ready for any emergency. Had he neglected "dead lights," "fore scuttle," and "upper yards," she never would have righted, for raisins grow heavy when water-soaked, and a vessel, under all the circumstances, could not have righted by cutting away her masts. He knew that our doom was the bottom of the ocean, or our bodies would be food for sharks, if she was not on her feet before the sea began its mountainous ravings again.

We found our cargo in splendid order on discharging it in New York. Weather cleared up, the gale abated, and now let us return to our present voyage.

Plenty of fish, plenty of wind, but on the coast we got soundings off Chincoteague Shoal, rigged our long geer for codfish. Hove to a half hour, and caught all we wanted; squared away with wind southwest; made the highlands, but before we got a pilot the wind popped out northwest and cold; were obliged to heave to, and drifted off to southward of the Gulf Stream. Wind backed round; headed her up for the Hook again; got

soundings off Barnegat; wind southwest; everything
set; came up with Sandy Hook; wind came out again
northwest at midnight, held us three days, and off she
went again; came up the third time, got hold of the
light at Sandy Hook, about 9 o'clock P. M. and no pilot;
wind northeast, light; indications of another nor'wester;
plumped her into the horse-shoe; skipper determined
not to be blown off again; overhauled a good scope of
both cables (hemp) and just as the prelude to the nor'-
wester struck us; we found four fathoms water; let go
both anchors; paid out to the better end; let fly everything; clued up, and had every sail "furled" but the
main top-sail, clued it up, hauled out the "earings," six
of us on the yard, Sam and the second Mate at the yard
arm; the latter outside; I was in the act of hauling up
the "dog's ear" when the nor'wester pounced on us, and
as my body was leaning over the yard it gave the sail a
twitch, took me clean over the yard, and as I went I
caught the reef tackle, hung by the right hand, and,
without a good grip, should have dropped overboard
clear of the vessel; but while the boy hung in that position he felt Sam's hand in his collar, and you may depend
he brought me up till I fastened to the "lift" and got
position again on the yard. It was so dark that we
could not see one another, nor could we hear. All
necessary remarks and exclamations from Sam were
reserved till we were all snug, and as we gathered
around the old galley, with a pot of grog, the vessel riding out the gale, Sam said to me: "Massa Charley,
u'ze a charmed chicken; u'ze may be hanged, but
u'ze nebber will be drowned." Sam was my trusty
body-guard, not only this voyage, but many others, and

in the intervals made his home in the family. He finally withdrew from the sea, and sighing for the "iron pots" and "skimmers," was installed as cook in a nice little brick building attached to the alms house, equally as happy as in his palmy days. He would not eat the bread of idleness, preferring his old occupation, and in the absence of the writer and family from New Haven, Sam's account with this world was closed at the age of 45. "*Sit tibi terra levis*," "Light lie the earth on thee." But to resume our voyage. We were in the "horse-shoe," riding out the "nor'wester," with "best bower" anchor "backed" with the "kedge," where she lay till morning; took a pilot and went to the city; making the passage in fifty-six days from Sicily. Fruit in fair order.

Remark Special.—This has been quite an eventful voyage, it certainly has to the writer; for had not his two guardian angels constantly hovered over him, I mean the skipper and old Sam, we never could have given you this narrative, and I should not have been placed in the position to render "honor to whom honor is due."

Advice.—Don't send a boy to sea in the hands of unprincipled men, in order to effect a cure of the "14-year-old fever," for generally it is a failure. Pick out the Peter Storer *kind*, and your boy, if bright, will make a man, and if with a grateful heart, and he cannot express it "*viva voce*," perhaps before he arrives at the age of 73, he will publish it in a book, and scatter the facts of his treatment broadcast. This voyage certainly was a compound of gales, calms, dangers, escapes, fun and frolic.

6

CARD.—Summer Boarding at Short Beach, Branford, Conn. Stages three times a day to and from New Haven. Opens June 1st—till November. Price $10 per week.

C. F. HOTCHKISS.

CALIFORNIA IN 1849.

Two sons on the way, Dec. 1848—Ship Orpheus—Passage by steamer
Crescent City, Sept. 1849—Death and Burial at Sea—Gold the gen-
eral topic with 500 Passengers—Touched at Havana—Arrival at
Chagres—Miserable Hole—Constant rains and excessive heat—
Effects of Gambling—Boatmen and Canoes—Alcaldi—Mutiny—
Capt. Henry Thompson of East Haven—Good Pluck—At Crusus—
Demand for Mules—Advice of an American—My mule Americanus
—Dead and balky Mules—Entered the gorge left foot first—Rains
and Mud—Beautiful Scenery—Lizards and Snakes—Route for Treas-
ure—Large transfers for ages—Beef by the yard—Sylvester Potter's
Horses—Safe arrival at Panama—Affection for Americanus—U. S.
Hotel—Scene in Cockpit—Sam's remark on "Consistumcy"—Bound
up the Coast—Steamer Panama, Capt. Bailey—Touched at Mazatlan,
Acapulco, and San Diego—Arrived at San Francisco—Breakfast on
Shore, $3.00—Scene at Happy Valley—Opened business same day
—No Vegetables—Scurvy—Bread at the front door free—Large
arrivals—Wm. Fuller sick—Arrival of brig Ann Smith, Capt. Bowus
—Scenes at Post Office—Gambling Hells—Vigilant Committee—Cur-
tain lifted—No Females—No time to lose—Store corner Sansom
and Jackson sts., rent $32,500—Butter $1.00 a pound—Moved to
Stockton—Safe Deposit—Vigilant Committee—A Woman arrived—
Warned by the Committee to leave—Scaffold and four graves at its
foot—Sick—" Vamoosed the Ranch "—Nice trip down the Coast—
Arrived safe at home—Account Current—Pope's Essay on Gold
Hunting.

THE author having fitted out his two sons, Henry and Charles, for California, they left New York by steamer " Crescent City," December 23d, 1848; crossed the Isthmus to Panama, from which place they reported themselves as waiting conveyance to San Francisco. After considerable delay they took passage in a small craft, unseaworthy and with miserable accommodations; suffered many privations, and through many risks at last arrived at San Francisco, and went immediately to the mines. Much anxiety was felt for their fate, and on the eve of my departure to look after them, we had advices as above, but not stating their destination from San Francisco. I selected 150 kegs (15,000 lbs.) choice butter; put in brine, placed each keg in another package, filled that also with brine, made up an invoice of other goods, shipped them by ship Orpheus from New York, consigned to myself. Among the goods were an old iron safe, of no particular value here, but, as will appear, of great value in California. It was about three feet square, no obstructions inside, with lid on top. Considerable many passengers went in the Orpheus round Cape Horn from New Haven—for which vessel I was the agent at that place. Your humble servant left New York by steamer Crescent City for Chagres, Sept. 15th, 1849, with a great crowd of gold-seekers, a singular compound of men, and but five women—in which both ladies and gentlemen were extremely scarce. If I touch any person's toes in this broad remark, you are at liberty to class me as you choose, though I think you cannot deny the truth of my assertion, if you were one of the 500 passengers on that trip. Gambling, rum and

oaths were the circulating medium the whole trip, morning, noon and night.   Gold was the absorbing topic of
conversation.   The day previous to our sighting the isl-
and of Cuba, where we were to touch for mails, one of
the number was brought on deck, laid on a board in the
waist of the ship near the quarter boat, with a view to
burial.   One of the passengers, with a cigar in his
mouth, stood at the head of the corpse, prayer book in
hand, the body, except the head, was placed in a piece
of old canvas, having about 100 lbs. of coal at the feet;
the skipper touched the engineer for a slow, the board
was pointed about forty-five degrees depression from the
ship's rail, the man of the prayer book took his cigar
from his mouth, and held it by the thumb and fore finger,
read a few short sentences, the national colors were
already up "to truck" and had been since 8 o'clock in
the morning, the ship not yet lost her steerage way,
when the man with the book cried out: "Launcho!!"
and the body slid from the board, a few bubbles
remained on the surface a moment, and the ship was on
her course again.   No notice was given of the intended
ceremonies; the colors gave no evidence of sympathy;
the ship did not lose her "way;" no notice was given
about the ship, nor were the gambling parties in any
way disturbed, and I asked myself: "If such scenes are
enacted on the Atlantic, what shall we witness on the
Pacific?"

   We touched at Havana, exchanged mails, and in due
time arrived at Chagres, a low, miserable town, of
thirty thatched huts, and the passengers got on shore as
best they could, in miserable shore canoes, under an old
roll of the Caribbean Sea, in which several were

swamped.   Chagres at this time was poorly prepared for
the immense emigration, and with half the canoes
required to transport them up to Crusus.   No eating
houses or saloons, in an extremely low latitude, and every
one who had not gambled away his money and ticket
for up the coast, anxious to get away from the miserable hole.   Our little party of four having had some experience in roughing, concluded a bargain with two
brawny natives to pole us through to Crusus, took them
before their alcalde (justice), paid the bill, conditioned
that they should lose no time on the way, they to feed
themselves, four hours per twenty-four given for rest,
and forfeit a flogging if they did not perform.   A wise
and good arrangement, as it proved, for the rascals
mutinied on us the next morning, and refused to go forward unless we gave them food.   We remonstrated,
took possession of the craft ourselves, shoved her off
shore, held by a pole well down in the mud, and waited
events.   Four Yankees, with each a pistol, on even
ground, against two natives, stark naked, was considerable odds in our favor, and we intended to keep it.   Soon
a passing canoe, with a single native, came drifting
down, to whom we beckoned.   He was a mongrel, and
carried quite a jolly countenance, and a native of Crusus,
with a spattering of mixed Congo and English.   We
stated our complaint against the mutineers, referred him
to them, and on hearing their story he decided against
them, and yet they refused to go.   By this time our
patience became exhausted, when Captain Henry Thompson, of East Haven, took his revolver from under his
shirt, we cast off the line, and our friend Thompson gave
it to them in tall Spanish, with a pistol pointed sharp at

the leader; but they gave in, and at it they went. At the next village we called down their alcalde, made our complaint and our fears of another outbreak; he heard their story, and if ever a native of the Isthmus got "Jesse," these men took it in double doses. We found this alcalde's supervision worked to a charm, for the "critters" behaved themselves the rest of the voyage. On we went in our little dug-out, difficulties all adjusted, cramped up in sitting posture, with an occasional landing to boil coffee, of which we gave the mutineers all they wanted—and thus in all we occupied three days and nights, amid the rain, shine and heat of this extreme latitude. The natives, with their songs and hoots, as they approached the villages, and the answers returned gave them good cheer. During the day the scenery was truly delightful. Parrots of various kinds, and paroquets, with their constant chattering in their flight across the river, monkeys occasionally in the trees, of all sizes, only of one kind; it was no uncommon thing to see a mother and her young huddled together apparently in fright at the encroachments of the gold-hunters, and instead of fleeing from danger, would climb a tree on the river bank, within shooting distance, and scold at the passer-by. Immense quantities of flowers on the edge of the river, the great lazy alligator would occasionally slide off the bank, and a world of smaller sizes on sticks and stones, were really frightful. The Chagres River appeared to be full of these venomous creatures.

On my trip down this river there were perhaps 100 canoes in requisition for passengers, many of whom not desiring to arrive in Chagres before daybreak, hauled up at a village three miles above. We came down late, and lay on the outside the fleet, made fast, and lay down for sleep. The moon was up, with a clear sky. I was awakened several times by a swash at the side of the canoe, and I raised up, stretched out my head, command-ing a view of the swell of the canoe, the rays of the moon showing young alligators, their hind parts in the water the whole length of the canoe, and the surface of the water was teeming with them; I was quiet for five minutes, when giving the canoe a sudden roll, they all returned to their native element. But my sleep for the night was minus, and I rejoiced that to-morrow I should be well out of sight if not mind of the Chagres River— its loathsome atmosphere and venomous reptiles. But I was doomed to witness a more vivid scene in the morn-ing. We moved opposite on the river to make up our morning's meal. I was the first ashore. Fronting me appeared a little alcove, having a beautiful grass plot of five rods square, nicely shaded with vines and shrubs, but literally alive with snakes, lizards and guanas. It appeared to me that I stood before a moving panorama of reptiles. I was nearly paralyzed at the sight. The snakes were of various sizes and color, and some ten feet long. They made as sudden a retreat as I did. The lizards covering bushes and shrubs, would retreat only as I advanced; in size from five to twelve inches, striped, brown, yellow, and red. My blood apparently ceased to flow, and it required some effort to rouse myself, and once in the canoe, I never left her till alongside the steamer for New York. I have ever since pondered in my mind, why this great convention of reptiles? why should the "boa" congregate with the little lizard? or the poisonous rattle with the guana? and I have never

satisfactorily solved these questions. Could it be that
the gathering was to consider the recent encroachments
of the gold-seekers, where perhaps six months before the
first human footstep touched that soil? Our readers
must remember that the Chagres River has been used
thousands of years for the transport of treasure, and seldom for a passenger, until the rush for California.

Crusus is the only place on this river giving evidence
of antiquity or civilization; the arrangements for the
transportation of treasure over the mountains to Crusus
and thence by canoe to ship at Chagres. Panama has
been the receiving warehouse for treasure ages ago, yes,
a thousand years or more before gold was discovered in
California, by the American people. It did not require
an army of soldiers to convoy it in its transit, any more
than it does now. It was brought to Panama, consigned to old established houses to forward; they sent
it on the backs of mules, through the mountain gorges,
under charge of a leading muleteer, to Crusus, with his
half-dozen drivers; there transferred to canoes, with but
one man in each to paddle it down to ship, but in 1848
a warehouse was built at Chagres, and now an agent is
kept there to transship. Formerly it was kept in Panama, till notice came of the ship's readiness to receive it.
The European monarchs and money-changers have during the palmy days of the old city of Panama, received
treasure through this channel, and are yet doing the
same thing. The night that the author rested at Crusus, in 1849, a train of fifty mules came in from Panama,
and unloaded the treasure contained in wood boxes of
suitable sizes, inclosing a tin box; and in conversation
with the consignee, he said not one dollar of it came

from California, but it was from Peru and other mining countries, and that for ages it had come through successive forwarding houses; he had done it all his days, then 60 years old, through his guardian in infancy, and back through his father, and his father's father also. We found Crusus quite a neat village, with a cleanly, neat, and honest people. Not well supplied with plum pudding and oyster sauce, but quite a sufficiency of Mexican beef, cut in strips, sun-dried, and sold by the yard. Monkey and guana were quite plenty and palatable, when a man is hungry, provided he does not see his toes, and these are left on in cooking, as evidence of their purity. Their coffee is good. The men are all schemers for money, and yet are honest. They carry tremendous chests and trunks on their heads, through the gorges to Crusus. The village is a dance house from dusk to midnight. The banjo is their favorite instrumental music, always accompanied by the female voice only. Your baggage put in the hands of the men at either Panama or Crusus for transit, is as safe as with the owner. The hotel was a horrid place in 1849, both in its eating and sleeping department—the latter, instead of the neat, clean South American hammock, consisted of bunks, full of vermin. Any person who should happen to require a lodging, could, if of cleanly appearance, obtain from the citizens a neat, cozy hammock swung in the open doorway, free from filth or vermin, for "duce rialis" (twenty-five cents), and see the dancing free. On my return trip the same hotel existed under the same administration, but experience being a good schoolmaster, we respectfully declined, and found better sleeping, without the accompanying torture of vermin.

But let us return to our departure from Crusus to Panama, through the gorges, for the mules are ready, and as a body much resemble the horses that our worthy citizen, "Sylvester," formerly dealt in, "none worth over ten shillings"—one of which I sold as auctioneer in New Haven for seventy-five cents, having advanced the worthy owner two dollars on it the day before. Sylvester was in the audience; State street was blocked up by the people, and always was at the sale of a horse, whether good, bad, or indifferent. The creature sold after much effort, for seventy-five cents, amid many cheers and some hisses. After getting a quiet audience, I said: "Gentlemen, this horse was sold for account of 'Sylvester,' under an advance of two dollars; please help me make up the account sales, for it seems to be on the wrong side of Daboll." One of the audience as suddenly as a clap of thunder, cried out: "Gentlemen, I propose that the auctioneer pay 'Sylvester' the seventy-five cents, and guarantee the purchaser that the 'old rip' lives till he arrives at his stable, giving him twenty minutes lee way. Are you ready for the question? Those in favor will say aye"—when the whole street responded in the affirmative, and your humble servant did as requested, paid the seventy-five cents, and bargained with the purchaser that he should have the animal without pay, if he would get him out of the street in two minutes. Well, these mules, financially, were like "Sylvester's" horses at New Haven—only that the Crusus mules were immediately absorbed, and it was found that the demand far exceeded the supply. Current price ten dollars for the ride to Panama—no reclamation on either side if he died on the journey. Acting

on a hint given by a railroad official, then surveying the
route for the Panama road, I rested for the crowd to
mount, when he turned to a native, told him my wants,
and to bring up his "Americanus," a large, beautiful
animal, with a splendid Mexican outrig, for which I
gladly paid him fifteen dollars, thanked my friend for his
kindness, and after receiving instructions for the mule's
care in Panama, I started with perfect assurance of my
safety on the trip—I covered the rear of the great cavalcade, passed a dozen mules on the balk, and some
floundering in mud holes. At the entrance of the first
gorge in the mountain, about a mile from the hotel, I
found several animals that refused to enter, while Americanus stepped square up to the work, entered the gorge
en miltair, left foot first, and never stumbled through
the route. These passages through the gorges are only
of sufficient width for a pack animal, and on entering
them from either end, a signal of a loud whistle or hoot
of the man in charge of the train is given, and answered
by the other, and the party omitting to give this notice,
if met in the gorge, must back out. The reader will
understand that these gorges are more or less circuitous,
quite uneven, varying in height from eight to twenty
feet, ascending and descending with foot marks made by
the animals from three to six inches deep, depending on
the hardness of the rock, and evidently this rough and
uncouth road has been used for many ages. The soil
between these gorges is extremely muddy in the season
of rain, and it is in these places where we realize the
value of an able mule. Many of the poor animals here
flounder and die; the riders must then foot it to Panama. "Americanus," with the reins untouched, would

pick his way through the mud, always enter a gorge left foot first, would make no halts but for water and grass, and in good heart carried me through to Panama and of his own accord, landed me at the United States Hotel, just at sunset, where I sat by his side, gave him bread and grass to his heart's content, and with a good rubbing down, kissed his homely face, bid him good-bye, and, as ordered in Crusus, turned him adrift to find his regular quarters in Panama. No animal without a muleteer is allowed to enter a gorge. They find a home at both ends of the route.

I turned to the hotel for my own quarters. The people continued to arrive till midnight—some on foot, weary, wet, and drunken. I consider that my investment of fifteen dollars was one of the best I ever made. Long live "Americanus." One incident that occurred in Panama worth relating, and we will "up the coast," where it seems as if all the world were bound. It was Sunday; while sitting at the hotel I noticed a church edifice directly opposite, on the steps of which was a colored boy with a splendid large Spanish game cock, to which he was fastening a pair of fine pointed gaffs. On inquiry of our landlord, I found the animal and boy were the property of the priest then officiating at the altar inside the church, and at 12 o'clock the services would close, and a grand fight would come off at the cockpit, six doors below, in which the priest would be "chief cook and bottle-washer"—seats free. At the time appointed I covered the rear of the procession, the boy, the game cock, and his reverence at the head, and entered the cock pit, under cover and in form like an ampitheater. About 300 persons were present, under no order or control, everybody had their say, and on the whole " a scene of confusion worse confounded," bedlam let loose, and in which his reverence was as active and noisy as the rest. The only rule (said my interpreter), which they agree to enforce, is, " that no person shall enter the pit during a fight." Money passed to the person in the rostrum quite freely, but the chatter and swearing continued without any intermission, and finally a pair of fowls were let in through the trap doors, each with steel gaffs on, and without any ceremony, at it they went—result, one dead, the other bleeding from the neck—several matches were made and closed—but your humble servant had no relish for such cruel scenes, but was much more interested with the audience, for by this time they were so clamorous that a field fight was in prospect, several clenches occurred, but results were not as plainly visible as in the case of the feathered tribe, for I soon found they were all great cowards, and made more " fuss than feathers." These men were all well dressed in white, the rig consisted mostly of slippers, white half-hose, linen pants and shirts, with a light straw hat; every one of them as clean as if just out of a band-box or laundry; but they were an excitable, nervous, boyish race—natural born cock-fighters and gamblers, all smoking splendid cigars, but what they lacked in fighting, they made up in confused ranting. But to close. His reverence was now getting up his match; he was plump six feet tall, of a sharp visage, dressed in black bombazine mantle, and black chapeau, black silk hose, and tight serge gaiters, and if never active before, was now truly " the biggest toad in the puddle," made the most noise, and swore more than any other man in the party. The two birds were let into the arena, amid continuous shouts and screams enough to frighten the evil one himself, if not the two roosters. As before stated, I was intent on the audience not in the pit, until the first slash, I saw the " dominie" jump into the pit for his bird, but it was too late, his throat was cut clean open,—he looked the picture of despair, took his dead bird and boy and walked away, minus, as my interpreter said, sixteen doubloons, and I trust a wiser and a better man, though the next Sunday he was burning incense at the altar of the same church. I seated myself on the shady verandah of my hotel, and remembered an expression of my good old cook, Sam Chase, when standing at the door of a dance house at Malaga, Spain, where rum flowed freely, and the priests drank and danced till drunk, he exclaimed: "Gorra mighty, Massa Charley, what kind of consistumcy is dis?"

The steamer Panama was ready, her passengers got on board as best they could, and we left for San Francisco, or rather, those of us who had not sold or gambled away our money or tickets. The ship was cleanly and under good discipline and command of Captain Bailey, whose orders were to touch off and on at Mazatlan, at Acapulco for coal, and San Diego for passengers, and then for San Francisco, but to use up twenty-one days on the passage. Nothing of interest occurred during the passage, and we arrived the twenty-first day, all well. I landed next morning, foot of Jackson street, and entered an eating room on Montgomery, ordered cup of coffee, two eggs, and beef steak, no butter, paid $2.50, and consoled myself that I had 15,000 pounds of choice butter in the ship Orpheus, which somebody

would be obliged to pay one dollar a pound for. I stepped out on the street—everything was in a crude state;
I spent a portion of the day in the examination of San
Francisco as it then was. At Happy Valley I found
about 200 people, "squatters," some in tents, some in
crockery hogsheads and dry-goods boxes, as their shelter. It was sufficient for their purpose, if the head was
protected from the storm, while their legs were left out.
What better could they do? A few buildings on the
Plaza had been roughly thrown together. One public
house, one old "adobe" shanty, the rest used as gambling houses. Lumber, if to be found, was worth $1,000
per one thousand feet. All vessels arriving were boarded
for this necessary article. Cotton goods and tacks were
wanted for tents, as a substitute, the latter two dollars a
paper: Long boots were in great demand at fifty dollars; bread, pork and nails were plenty; molasses, none;
sugar, any price demanded; Mexican beef and salmon
plenty; flour, forty dollars. People constantly arriving
by vessels, and streets quite lively. Well, the day was
far spent, and it was time for me to make a dive for a
shelter. A plain board shanty was being erected on the
corner of Montgomery and a street leading to the Plaza.
The roof was on, but no partitions. I bargained for ten
feet square on first floor for 150 dollars per month, to be
put in order, and I put in possession in one hour, for
which I paid the gold, and it was quite amusing to
notice the way that nails were crowded into boards.
Everything in the carpenter line was "by the job"—and
true to the bargain, my shelter was finished, and at dusk
I rolled into my bunk, a blanket for a bed, and slept as
soundly as a king till morning. "Cash paid for every-

thing," was my chalk sign, and by 8 o'clock A. M. I was
an old resident, ready for business. Vessels were constantly arriving, and from them we gleaned many articles, never questioning price. The cry was, goods!
goods!! from every quarter. "Big-sized boots" were
my favorites. I found three cases, and before night all
sold at fifty dollars a pair. Anything portable was
what I aimed at, because ten feet square could not hold
much coarse staples. Tacks for tents were another favorite, and every vessel would spare a few. The simple
rule in merchandising was, pay the price named, and
ask what you choose. The influx of people was a curiosity, many of whom were dumped ashore from vessels
without money or food. Pilot bread in large quantities
had fortunately been shipped from Boston, and this gave
some relief, but vegetables were out of the question.
The want of these necessities caused much sickness.
Scurvy and diarrhœa were the universal complaints;
every potato and onion that ships would part with was
hoarded up for the sick; no sound man could obtain one
for his own eating. A cask of bread and barrel of pork
stood at the door of every merchant, free to the
sick.

The miners began to arrive from the mines to recruit.
They had gold and scurvy both—the former worthless,
without a potato or an onion. These two articles were
the only antidote for their complaint, and it was amusing to see with what avidity they would scrape them
with a knife, costing half their weight in gold. This
state of things was soon remedied by the arrival of vessels from Chili; but for six months these articles sold for
one dollar the pound. With onions or potatoes raw, the

7

worst case of scurvy could be cured in ten days. But I must not give the reader much more of this melancholy picture.

It was calculated that the increase of population in San Francisco was over 1,500 persons average per day from February 1st to June 1st, 1850, and that over 400 vessels of various nations and sizes, in May, were at anchor in the bay, deserted by their crews, but generally with a single ship-keeper on board. Had there been a sufficiency of lumber and carpenters in the market we could with truth say, " A city could be built in a day." But trade went on swimmingly, and with good margins.

I was comfortably surprised one morning to welcome my old neighbor, Wm. Fuller, Esq., having arrived from Sacramento to recruit, and bringing me news from my two sons, who were then with his friends on the " American fork"--and in my little quarters of ten feet square he was made as comfortable in his severe sickness, and during the season of rains, as we could control. His was the chronic diarrhœa, caused by exposure in the Sacramento salmon fishing. Friend Fuller will tell you of his narrow escape and suffering, but now hale and hearty, dealing largely piscatorially on Long Wharf, New Haven, Ct. It was evident that Mr. F. was not improving in health with the crude accommodations under my roof, and the constant chilly rains of the season, and I solicited Captain William Bowns, then lying at anchor in the bay, to take Mr. F. on board his vessel, being sanguine that it would save his life, and the writer is happy to place on record the hearty response received from the Captain, who immediately welcomed him on board, gave him every attention and care, under which Mr. Fuller immediately began to mend, and in three weeks went on his way rejoicing, a well man.

I purchased the cargo of Captain Bowns, and paid the bill in full; never had a dispute with him with regard to reclamations for shorts or damage, but found him to be the same noble-hearted man as in boyhood, a kind, generous play and schoolmate of mine all my younger days, from three years old, and with whom the writer enjoyed many a "piscatorial" excursion in middle life. All our intercourse at San Francisco was genial, pleasant and friendly, and I challenge the world to find one who more keenly mourned his decease than I did, not excepting his wife. It is said that "murder will out in time," and this is a good opportunity to prove the application of the old adage. After the decease of Captain William Bowns, the author was considerably annoyed by reports emanating from one who stood high in the family of the Captain, that "she was made poor by reason of C. F. Hotchkiss having CHEATED the Captain out of the cargo sold him in San Francisco."

Remarks.—The only cargo bought by the writer of Captain Bowns was that alluded to above, and for the payment of which I hold a receipt in full, and, furthermore, I respectfully refer my friends or enemies, who swallowed and repeated the unqualified lie to my injury, to Charles Peterson, Esq., President of the New Haven Security Insurance Company, the owner of said vessel and cargo, who will tell you that the good Captain did not own a penny of the cargo, nor did he in the settlement of that voyage report any balance due from your humble servant. My quarters in my little office on Montgomery street were too strait, and I rented a two story building

in course of erection, located on the flats, foot of Jackson
street, sixty feet square, the lower floor for goods, three
doors opening to the sea, a dock, on the south side for
landing goods and passengers. The upper story was
converted to bunks, three tiers high, making about 100
bunks. The approach to the city was by a bridge. It
was the first building erected below Montgomery street,
and its rent was 32,500 dollars per year, payable
monthly in advance, privileged to vacate in four months.
Here we had a good, roomy place for goods. Lodgings
one dollar each person, they finding bedding. I boarded
many friends, lodged many strangers, making it a rule
never to turn the poor away. Vessels continued to
arrive. Lumber fell to 500 dollars per thousand; buildings rose in every direction like magic. Men off a long
voyage were dumped ashore like cattle, at least 100
miles from the mines, and passage to Stockton or Sacramento twenty-five dollars. Stout hearts quailed,—the
robust and the strong were the first to succumb. My
store, without rum (thank God), was the great thoroughfare for the living and the dead. It was difficult to tell
whether less or more of the sick came from the mines or
landed from vessels. Scurvy from the mines and ship
fever from the vessels.

Our only law was a Vigilance Committee—they not
considering the dead and dying as coming within their
jurisdiction. Gold, gold, gold, could well be the epi-
taph of thousands. Thus far for the dark side, not half
told. The bright side to me was the arrival of my two
sons—both sick—but vegetables were getting plenty,
and with the care and council of Doctor Beers, formerly
of New Haven, Charles, the youngest, recruited suffi-

ciently, and by advice of the doctor was sent home in company with Mr. W. J. Clark, of Southington, who kindly volunteered to care for him. Henry remained with me.

The ship Orpheus arrived safe, and her invoice paid a round margin; butter on its arrival was one dollar per pound. The busy scenes of life began to tell on me. Those strong, cold winds of San Francisco were too much, and I heeded the admonition, began to prepare for a removal to Stockton, but before I go let me describe the scenes on the Plaza. Post office first— every day a string of people three deep, twenty rods long, waiting a chance at the delivery. Two days often passed before the party at the rear could get a chance at the window; many times have I seen a line forming in the night, to insure a chance next day; five dollars was often paid for a chance near the window, the party retiring must go to the rear. The office facilities were of course imperfect. These men were mostly miners, and they represented all their friends in the mines, and these were easily distinguished by a bag of gold, large or small, slung over the neck, the bag resting in their bosom. The newly arrived generally had on a good shirt, but the others more likely no shirt at all, an unshaven, care-worn, hard-looking set of men, of all countries, nations, and tongues. Some good natured, some ugly looking, and an occasional tall, lank, gray-eyed Vermonter, and down to the poor Chilian, half-naked. At the side of this string could be seen 500 to 1,000 new-comers, seeking information of the mines and how to get there, and an occasional recognition of friends would take place. Then those who had passed the rubicon were scattered in all directions, reading letters from "sweet-hearts and wives." On the opposite side of the Plaza were the gambling hells, in full blast, with piles of gold, which the uninitiated would buck against in vain.

These scenes, mixed with the hundreds in the streets of poor, sickly and emaciated men with scurvy and diarrhœa, more like moving ghosts, was sufficient to make one cry out, "All for gold." Yes, all this and more, and yet not a female to be seen, except, perhaps, an occasional Digger squaw. This was the panorama of the winter of 1850 and spring of '51. Oh! what degradation for gold!

But let us look around near the corner of the Plaza, where the national colors are flying, and where the Vigilance Committee, in the absence of all statute or territorial law, take in hand the administration of justice, and where it swiftly followed arrests. Nothing else would seem to answer the purpose, for if they were without organization, our lives would not be worth a brass farthing. No crowd of anxious information-seekers or curiosity-hunters are ever seen in that room, though the national emblem tails to the breeze night and day. It is empty now, but perhaps in half an hour a private duplicate key will admit eight men of business with a tiler, but there will be no formal crier to open the court. The gavel strikes the table, and the prisoner is brought in from a side door, the witnesses confront him; there is no sick juror to wait for, the judges are business men, there are no pettifoggers to worry the judge; time is precious in San Francisco now; men have immense rents to pay; they move quick; there is no superfluity of words; jurors cannot be bribed nor witnesses befog-

ged. The story is told, and it is told to honest men—
men without a salary—men who are sick of the intrica-
cies of law, and men who will administer justice, though
the heavens were on fire. "What is your opinion, gentlemen?" The answer comes by signs. "The prisoner
is guilty." There is no long roll of talk from the bench,
to harrow up the soul of the guilty wretch. He is told
his doom; he is not (vide the Spanish inquisition) put
to the rack in order to extract information as to his
accomplices. He is plainly told what he knows to be
true, "You are guilty of murder. You have twenty
minutes to prepare for death." The scaffold is in the
room—the time is up—he swings, a sharp piece of steel
enters his heart—the tiler does his duty, and the body
is taken to "the hill" in the evening, where all the dead
are buried. The flag still floats; the protectors of the
people's interests have resumed their business, and for
the sake of example, it may or may not be said that
another murderer has paid the penalty of his crime, but
his name is never mentioned.

Now, reader, I have closed my interest at San Francisco, which I found to be a very easy matter. New-
comers were plenty, and away for Stockton. The climate and surroundings being much more congenial to
my constitution and feelings, but I shall remember the
howling morning winds that with a cold, dense fog, roll
over the city of San Francisco. The trade of Stockton
is mostly with muleteers, who run trains of pack mules
with supplies for the miners.

The old steamer Sutter made regular trips from San
Francisco three times a week; fare twenty-five dollars.
Stockton then had about 1,200 inhabitants, and only one

female, except three poor, degraded Digger squaws; with five wood buildings, the other shelter was tents. The wood buildings were occupied for gambling, where "monte" was the favorite game. The town was regularly laid out, with a street leading up from the landing seventy feet wide. Goods were generally displayed in front of the tent in the street, exposed to view and thieves, during four months of the year, without danger from dews or rains. Lots then occupied on this street cost 5,000 dollars cash. The old iron safe, before mentioned, was now in its position, it being but the third in the place. It was a cheap sheet iron safe, and yet its shape was just suited to not only our wants but also the miners and muleteers, each of whom in coming from the mines would deposit their bag of gold—the former to recruit, and the latter to purchase goods. We seemed to be the treasury for the whole country, and during the time we were there we never weighed or counted a single bag, and never had a word of difficulty with a depositor. Not a bag during the time was sealed. It was marked with the owner's name, and it was no uncommon thing to have on hand 150 bags, valued at from twenty to one thousand dollars each. We made no charge for deposits, and the acquaintance and reputation in the mines brought a large trade. The muleteers, with from five to thirty pack mules, would arrive about noon, the head mule rode by the boss, carried the bag or bags of gold on the pommel of the saddle, and if for a large purchase, the assistant on the rear mule carried gold in the same way. The train would halt at our tent, the principal would take off the gold, lay it in the safe, hand us a list of his wants, to be ready to pack the

second day—not a word of price—if the articles were
not in the place, we could send by steamer Sutter; in
that case and that only, would he be satisfied to hold
over.   When all was ready, the mules would be at the
door; ask for the bill, take out his gold from the safe,
and weigh out the sum required, and away for the mountains.   Our tent was called the "cure-all," for we aimed
never to be short on onions or potatoes.   Ours was also
an exchange office, and those returning to the States
would exchange dust for coin.   Wholly unused to such
unlimited confidence, I trembled at the result at the
beginning, but in a fortnight's time became accustomed
so as to sleep soundly in my hammock, directly over the
old safe, with a right and left hand supporter under my
pillow.

Stockton had its Vigilant Committee, and in the middle of the street on an elevation, say about twenty rods
from us, they had erected a gallows, and at its foot were
four mounds of fresh-made graves.   Your humble servant was, soon after his arrival, by request of the Committee, made a member of that important arm of the law.
The jurisdiction of this Committee was unlimited, but it
generally refused to act in cases outside the township.
Society in Stockton was a curious compound.   Gold was
the only god it worshiped then.   The one white female
before named, was a lady commanding the respect of
every person in the place.   The Diggers were poor, miserable brutes.   My mule, "Americanus," that carried
me over the mountains to Panama, was a queen in comparison.   Men were, in the absence of society, slovenly
and undignified, and we naturally fell into these habits,
still (throwing your humble servant out), they were gen-

tlemen of integrity, noted for neighborly acts of kindness, and as prompt as the hand of time. There were no lazy ones in the settlement, and while at Stockton I never saw a person worse off for liquor, except the "Diggers." Notwithstanding the country was flooded with genuine Bordeaux brandy, in cases, three cargoes of which had been landed in San Francisco in 1848, at the instant the gold was discovered, the crews of the ships having left the vessels, and the whole was forced on the market at a song's price.

Woman was a curiosity, as was evidenced one day about 8 o'clock, when a great uproar was made, commencing at the landing, and gaining strength as the sound reached us; every occupant was in the street, the cheer was long, loud, and strong—and behold, it was a woman, backed on a beautiful horse, richly dressed in a long riding habit, a neat jockey cap, white feather, face highly painted, and she escorted by a man well dressed, also on a beautiful bay charger. The men swung their hats, and it was a universal cheer on cheer. On the 10th day after her majesty and her pimp went through this great and wonderful ovation, the Vigilant Committee, through their tiler, served a notice on them both to leave by the Sutter next day, without fail. The mandate was obeyed, and they took ten thousand dollars with them. I make no comment—the reader has the floor.

The climate at Stockton was beautiful. The plain extended twenty miles to the mountain—this was by one road, used entirely by miners and pack trains, and early in its being traveled was the scene of two murders and two robberies, of which fact the scaffold in Stockton bears testimony.

The writer was satisfied that chronic diarrhœa was no respecter of persons, and if life was worth more than gold, it was time for him to nurse his health, and with his son, Henry, after closing up our business, took steamer for home. We had a beautiful run down the coast; crossed the Isthmus, joined the steamer for New York, and arrived safe at New Haven, August 7th, 1850, with two good-sized bags of gold, showing a balance against the enterprize of $23,000.

The account stood thus:

To	Dr.
Cash outfit to California, including self and two sons	$7,000
Wear and tear, body, soul, and breeches	10,000
Privations (non-society)	5,000
Do., morning winds and fogs in San Francisco	2,000
Risk of life in various ways	10,000
"Rolling stone" process	5,000
	$39,000
	Cr.
By two bags gold, containing	$16,000
" balance to new account	23,000
E. E.	$39,000

New Haven, August 7th, 1850.   C. F. HOTCHKISS.

Pope speaks my sentiment relative to gold-hunting:

"To either India see the merchant fly,
 Scar'd at the spectre of pale poverty!
 See him, with pains of body, pangs of soul,
 Burn through the tropic, freeze beneath the pole!
 Wilt thou do nothing for a nobler end,

Nothing, to make philosophy thy friend?
To stop thy foolish views, thy long desires,
And ease thy heart of all that it admires?
Here, wisdom calls: 'seek virtue first, be bold!
As gold to silver, virtue is to gold.'"

CARD.--Summer Boarding at Short Beach, Branford, Conn. Stages three times a day, to and from New Haven. Open June 1st—till November. Price, $10 per week.

C. F. HOTCHKISS.

SAM PATCH'S LAST LEAP.

SAM was a noted character of the loafer species, his associate a black bear and a brandy bottle. His motto, " Some things can be done as well as others," was ever present with him, either printed in large letters, or at the end of his tongue. The good people of Rochester, N. Y., for many years after Sam's death, in 1829, were greatly averse to hear or say anything about this great hero. The Eastern world have heard the name, while the former knew him in person; for he could be seen walking with his bear through their streets, recounting his great exploit of jumping the falls of Niagara, and his promising to make his " last jump " at Genesee Falls. Sam aspired to no other honors than jumping, and had educated his companion, the bear, to the same beautiful feat of ground and lofty tumbling. He had frequently done the exploit at the Genesee, and safely; but it was, as he said, done quietly in order that he could get the " hang of the barn," but now he concluded to make a noise in the world and let the people of Rochester know that " some things could be done as well as others." His motto, his tongue and his bear were his sole capital, and on these he was determined to rally and " cut a swarth " in the world, and by calling the people to his "last jump" he would be "greatly enriched with honor and gold." He would then "go to Europe, jump all their falls and return rich." These were his views, freely expressed to his printers, Tuttle, Sprague and Sherman, where he selected large wood type, "Sam's Last Leap," for the heading of his poster, and his favorite motto, "Some things can be done as well as others," at the foot.

Sam having freedom among the rum shops and saloons, he and the bear during the three weeks of his announcement made calls once a day, brandy for Sam, and crackers with sugar on them for Bruin, all free. No one seemed disposed to annoy the pair, and it was asserted by Sam Drake and Joe Seely, both gentlemen of truth and integrity, that Sam's inwards were cased with oiled silk to prevent the hundred drinks which he took each day from eating through, and on Drake's being questioned as to the effect of brandy on his brain, he quickly replied that "Sam never had any," and added, "many people have a place for that necessary commodity, but poor Sam Patch was entirely minus, or, as might be better understood, *nullius filius.*" And yet, Sam knew enough to find Baker's horse shed on Buffalo street every night when the labor of the day was over, but friend Drake denied it and gave Bruin that honor.

The people had no idea that Sam wanted to commit suicide, although the bills would indicate otherwise. Nothing was said or done about putting a stop to the show. Everybody within the range of Ontario, Genesee, Wayne, or Monroe Counties were amused at the idea of witnessing the great feat, as was proved by their presence. Even the village of Rochester and its President, my worthy and valued friend, Joseph Medbury, Esq., never supposed such a thing could or would be done to interfere with the proceedings. The Rochesterites were so anxious to see the show that everyone but the halt, the lame, the blind, and those that were behind the bars on Jail street, under the care of Mr. Merchant, were there, babies and all. Both river banks above and below the falls, and every building near them were lined with people, and no doubt 50,000 people witnessed the scene. It was but a moment's job for any person to step into the Arcade, and with a reasonable affidavit made before his Honor Wm. S. Bishop, Justice, the performance would have been knocked higher than a kite, and Sam (if friend Drake's philosophy is disturbed) to-day might be an ambassador to the Ladrones.

Sam was a vagrant and everybody knew it. They knew he was drunk when he tied Bruin to the scaffold, and yet these squeamish old maids and wiseacres, not one of them made a move to either stop or protest against the proceeding. The author feels a little sore on this subject and has waited about fifty years to throw the lash, as the sequel will show. And those of you now alive who then figured in the abuse to the writer, will fully understand me without further explanation; but if not I will get up a lecture at Rochester on Sam Patch and his "last jump," admittance free.

By Sam's arrangement and selection, a scaffold was erected at the edge of the falls on the west side of the river, twenty-four feet additional above the falls. Sam selected eight persons, special and deputy constables, to solicit money from the people. He mounted the scaffold drunk and clamorous, turned to the east bank, vaunting and rattling off an incoherent mess of disconnected

words, with strong ill-shapen gestures and contortions of
body, twisting himself into all shapes, then suddenly
turned to the west, occupying by my watch five minutes,
not one word of which was heard above the falls by reason of the roar of the water, and in an instant, without
waiting to inflate his lungs, wheeled, facing the water,
and with both hands uplifted made the jump. At half-
way down his hands dropped to his side; his body,
forming a portion of a circle, struck the water on his
right side, the blow of which was sufficient to knock the
breath from his body, but there is no question that he
died in the air. Your humble servant was under the
falls and said to a friend at his side, He is dead. And
though raked for several days was never seen until three
months after, and then found at Carthage. The great
mass of people waited a few moments and turned away,
some with a tear of regret, others growling and ranting
everybody and everything, for "suffering the man to
commit suicide," while others, more prudent, went quietly
home to ponder over "Sam's last leap." When satisfied
that Sam had truly made his last effort, one of his companions dragged poor Bruin to the edge of the falls and
gave him a launch for his master. The bear, more wise
than his master, gathered himself in a heap, struck on
his haunches, went just under the surface, came up, gave
a good sneeze and made for the shore, where his new
master was waiting for him, and they left for parts un-
known—boon companions.

The persons holding the contributions paid for the
efforts made to obtain the body, gave a report to each
other, advertised for the heirs of poor Sam, afterwards
called a meeting of citizens at Christopher's Tavern,

Deacon Hawley in the chair. We desired advice as to the disposition of the funds, then amounting to about $300. About 100 citizens were present. Nothing was done but to abuse the poor officers. The good old Deacon held the meeting up to strict rules, and still they heaped the abuse, and your humble servant received a full share. The meeting broke up for want of order, without action. When Sam's body came to the surface we called another meeting, stating in the call that we proposed, as the body was now within our reach needing burial, to expend the funds in erecting a monument on the bank of the river to his memory, and that to the present no heirs had appeared. About seventy persons were present. After considerable cross-firing the question, " Shall a monument be erected ?" was negatived sixty to ten. A bitter feeling began to show itself; we were targets again. Finally a gentleman offered his remarks, saying, "I consider this whole matter a disgrace to our village. We have allowed a poor drunken fool to commit suicide right before our face and eyes, without making the least effort to prevent it. Our citizens should be thankful that time will outlive memory, and there was hope that the thing would be forgotten. It was as much your and my business to interfere as these officers, and though I appreciate the motive of these gentlemen in their offer to erect a monument and the efforts they have made to disburse the collections, but really, Mr. Chairman, were they to erect this monument, I should expect a similar scene as was witnessed at the Tower of Babel, and if these men escaped with their lives they would be extremely fortunate. I move you, sir, that the gentlemen bury the dead and make no more efforts to get shut of the money."

8

This compromise seemed to give satisfaction. The resolution passed unanimously, the eight parties in interest not voting.

Now, if your humble servant had not been so shamefully persecuted, he never would have resurrected the story of Sam Patch, and if the whole truth had been told to the people there would have been no necessity for any person either in or out of Rochester to call on an old salt of three score years and thirteen to come forth from his little snug harbor at Short Beach, Branford, Connecticut, and give information relative to "Sam's Last Leap."

CARD.—Summer Boarding at Short Beach, Branford, Conn. Stages three times a day to and from New Haven. Open June 1st till November. Price, $10 per week.

C. F. HOTCHKISS.

RESPECT TO AGED FISHERMEN.

THE rule among fishermen has been, "If too old to fish, and yet incline to go with the boys, you must take the middle thwart and cut bait for the party." This is good piscatorial law, except seating him on the middle thwart. I always give them the stern sheets. The reader would no doubt say, that when a man becomes an "old fogy" and can't fish, sea-legs all gone, it is no place for him in a boat. Not so, friend. These old fogy fishermen, as long as they can see a land-mark or a tide rip, or have the use of the tongue, are useful as well as ornamental. Useful as before mentioned, to cut bait and tell shark stories. Ornamental, in that their full flowing white hair answers as a signal to other boats to give us a good birth, a respect to old age, and beside, they make good ballast. It has been a privilege during my piscatorial life to take in my boat all the "old fogy" fishermen that had good eyesight and teeth, and some who were plump up to four-score years and ten, notwithstanding they could not walk, but required a "sky tackle" purchase to carefully get them in and out of the boat. My plan was to place the good old souls in the stern sheets (the seat of honor) give him the best gear, bait his hooks, make the end of his line fast to a cleat, "throw and haul" his line for him when he called for

help, always sit beside him and occasionally give his
line a nip, but if he could not hook the fish I would put
one on myself and let him run, and the old man would
get him in somehow. It was worth more than it cost to
see the wonderful effect on an old fisherman.   Oh, how
his eyes would sparkle and flash, and then hear him as
he hauled a fish, sing out, "Can't fish, ha! An old fogy
and can't fish, ha!" and I said to myself, Who would
refuse to give the old fogy fisherman one more chance at
his favorite amusement? It may be your lot or mine to
be an old fogy.   If mine, I have no doubt I shall be re-
warded in a measure, "inasmuch," etc., for if when your
humble servant shall be " laid up in ordinary," and can't
get into a boat, his friends will no doubt place him in a
nice easy chair in the shade of the old white oak tree,
his vision spanning Short Beach Bay on a sweep of the
horizon from W. to E. S. E., while he in a faint voice,
sings " Oh, vat a man I was once ! But I never was dat
man vat I has been for all."

Moral: Do not neglect the old fishermen while their
vision is good ; they may be too far gone to write a history of the past, or to get into a boat and fish, but generally if with a breath left, they can sigh for the " leeks
and onions," and tell a good fish story. Always tip your
beaver to an old fisherman and ask him if he has tried
" New Reef" the present season, and if he is poor in
purse hand him a dollar and ask him if he will go with
you to the " Cow and Calf" off Branford the first pleasant day.   Look him square in the eye and you will see a
tear gathering in the corner as clear as a choice diamond.
Poor old man, he feels the infirmities of age, but his
memory is roused and he replies, " Old Cow and Calf!

and then there's Branford Beacon, two miles to the east-ward, where I have fished in early days with Hotchkiss, he that 'catches all creation.' " See, the old man has re-newed his age. You have touched the right note. He is awake again. He has been a reader in his day, and reminds you that the day has come " when the keepers of the house shall tremble and the strong men shall bow themselves, and the grinders cease because they are few, and those that look out of the windows be darkened and the doors shall be shut in the streets, when the sound of the grinding is low, and he shall rise up at the voice of the bird, and all the daughters of music shall be brought low. Also when they shall be afraid of that which is high, and fears shall be in the way, and the almond tree shall flourish, and the grasshopper shall be a burden, and desire shall fail; because man goeth to his long home, and the mourners go about the streets; or ever the silver cord be loosed, or the golden bowl be broken, or the pitcher be broken at the fountain, or the wheel broken at the cistern. Then shall the dust return to the earth as it was, and the spirit shall return unto God who gave it."

CARD.—Summer Boarding at Short Beach, Branford, Conn. Stages three times a day to and from New Haven. Open June 1st, till November.

C. F. HOTCHKISS.

THE SERPENT OF THE SEA.

MY readers will no doubt agree with me about the testimony yet given to the world as to the existence of the Sea Serpent, Nahant, Cape May and Nantucket to the contrary, notwithstanding. The author in the Atlantic and Pacific waters has never been a witness for the snaky monster, though he has witnessed the gambols of the grampus and porpoise, with an occasional sight of a "humpback" on the far horizon on a calm day and a quiet sea, which sometimes would resemble the graphic description of a "Sea Serpent off Nahant," and yet I believe that such "critters" do exist in a more southern latitude. In conversation with my good, kind old skipper, Capt. Peter Storer, whom the world must believe, I drew from him the following :

"In 1806 the ship Baltimore, of Baltimore, owned by Billy Patterson, on entering Calcutta Bay, and off the island of Salone, with a light breeze, sighted on the weather bow an object resembling a large stake about four feet above the surface and distant about half a mile, on the move, with about equal speed of the ship, apparently intending to cross the bow. Having a heavy pair of four-prong grains, they were immediately rigged in a nine-thread rattling stuff and a full coil, by the skipper, Sylvanus Long, of Nantucket, who jumped into a plat-

form fastened on her bowsprit shrouds, and with a strong
cast put the grains through the creature just under the
surface. The spear came out of the socket, became tan-
gled among the spritsail-yard guys, the animal half out
water and making tremendous efforts to shake of the
grains, but they had too firm a hold, though the lanyard
parted and he went off to leeward on the surface with
the water in a perfect foam and was seen for a half hour
before he sank. On the log of the ship he is described
as an animal without scales, a large bright eye, about
twenty feet long, tapering from near the center to head
and tail, and was a foot in diameter eight feet from his
head. His body was plainly seen its full length and no
portion of it near the surface except as before stated.
It was in shape a perfect serpent, and in a region of salt
water of eighty fathoms deep. And further, the same
parties on the same day caught a herring hog from which
they extracted a dozen real genuine snakes, from one to
three feet long."

The reader will observe that all previous descriptions
of the sea serpent yet given us, and especially "off
Nahant," affirm that when he moves in the water he
represents a dozen or less hummocks on his back, or por-
tions of circles, thus asking us to believe that he could
get up a fair speed with the body in that position. I
pronounce it all a canard. Give us the Bay of Bengal
snake in preference, for his or her body was in a natural
position. Ask my old skipper if he advocates the affirmative on Sea Serpents.

THE inquiry often comes up as to the location of this snug watering place which has recently been brought into notice, and is now being built upon for summer residence. It lays about three miles east of New Haven Lighthouse, in the town of Branford, Conn., in a beautiful bay fronting Long Island Sound, and due north, about two miles from the "Cow and Calf" (rocks so famous in the estimation of our old fishermen).

When the author and Mr. George Gunn dropped an anchor here three years ago, they found a small number of neighbors who gave them the right hand of fellowship, sold part of their possessions at a fair price, and with but one road terminating at the sea, threw in their influence to induce the town of Branford to open a road leading westerly to East Haven and easterly to Double Beach and Branford Center. This work has been accomplished, and it surprises the world generally to witness the improvements in so short a time. Our little bay is in the form of a horse-shoe, protected on the north by elevated land regularly declining to the beach; westerly by high bluffs; southerly, opening the view of Long Island Sound from west to east, and easterly by a range of rocks visible at high water, overlooking the same to the horizon. On a promontory at the west chop of the bay are the beautiful residences of Messrs. Reynolds, Horton, Williams, Cory and Bristol. Fronting the sea on the east chop are the residences of Messrs. Wilcox, Rev. Simonds, the W. C. of Wallingford and Oneida, and Mrs. Hamilton, of Hartford, and, divesting the author of Me-gotism, he would say that, fronting the sea on the north are the residences of Messrs. Gunn, Miller, Clark, Jun., Church, Becket, Bradley, Hart, Doolittle, Clark, Sen., and Wm. J. Clark, Ives, Nichols, Crane, Coles, Marvin, Hartson, Hough, and though last, not by any means least, the cottage of the humble old fisherman and jolly author.   ☞ At your service.

But hark! what's up? Ah! yes, I understand. It's the signal from the Commodore of the "Rockland Park Navy," W. H. Reynolds, of the beautiful Nita, carrying his broad pennant signaling the fleet to "heave short." And casting my eye over Horton's Point, and under the lee of Darrow's Island, on which is the home of Captain Bailey and his good wife, I saw in perfect trim and line, the Sappho, Florence, Lillie, Venus, Pet, and Onward. It was the first rendezvous of the season, and the morning as clear as their white hulls by paint, and sails, by bleaching, could in man's ingenuity be made. Casting an eye seaward, everything betokened a white-ash breeze, but in the bay an occasional cat's-paw spent itself on the surface of the water, which otherwise was as smooth as glass. The little white "spike-tailed" gull had left his rookery down Sound, and made an occasional dive for a fish within speaking distance of the fleet. The tide by its rips on the outside reefs indicated flood, and with my glass pointed to Long Island shore, a spanking breeze about W. by S. was on his way. The com-

modore saw it, and in the twinkling of a codfish's eye
sent his "bos'n" in the little gig to each craft with the
message, "Have your reef gear ready! and make no
harbor unless stress of weather requires! round Branford Beacon and return." On the quarter seat to each
craft were one or more ladies, rigged *a la* sailor, dark
tight-fitting coat and brass buttons, small jockey hat
and no feathers—sails mutton-legged, no main boom to
knock the ladies on the head, no thumping of the heart
with fear, but full of courage; for it is a rule in this fleet
to "keep main sheet in hand." But let us return to the
Commodore, with his broad blue and red pennant tailing
to the first overshot breeze, spring on his cable, leading
aft, but stopped on a ring bolt with a yarn. The whole
code of signals he keeps within the fleet, but the author
caught the order "Pay off to port! let go! And with
a glorious wind the fleet was in the wake of the Nita,
going like scalded hogs. Beautiful sight, "free sheets,"
starboard tacks aboard, going ten knots an hour. Oh,
how the water did fly! The author was so well pleased
with the seamanship displayed by the lads that he never
intruded the question of "who rounded the beacon first?"
But he will throw up his colors and hat for the "Rockland Park Navy" any time.

"THROW A ROPE!"

ON the quarter rail of a taut-rigged vessel, be she large or small, you will notice a " belaying pin " on which is a coil of small rigging, the " better end " spliced to a " thimble bolt " at the under side of the rail. The other end has a small buoy of wood well secured, above which are knots every three fathoms. This neat little coil of rigging is a fixture and never for ordinary use. A strict disciplinarian and humane skipper would as soon think of starting on the voyage without a compass, as to omit casting his eye on both quarters of the ship for this simple apparatus, or sing out, " Let go your fast ！" while the gang plank is out. This piece of rigging is occasionally dropped overboard to remove " kinks " and re-coiled on the pin, but never stopped. It is so neatly laid when coiled that should the cry of "A man overboard " be heard, a good strong arm can throw it from the ship, unfolding itself in the air, without a snarl or kink. If no such cry is heard on board the ship, then the coil of rigging is useless.

In the winter of 1873, a young man, calling himself an Evangelist, having been recently converted at Philadelphia, came to New Haven and assumed the pulpit of the Howe Street Church. His preaching was apparently satisfactory to the people judging from the crowds who attended the services, and certainly there was reasonable evidence that many persons had become converted. Everything appeared to go on smoothly with the young man and his cause for a few months, when it was evident that his work could not be prosecuted in peace. Certain men who had been instrumental in placing him in the pulpit, without any church organization openly declared war against him, with the threat that he not only should vacate the pulpit but the city. This was in the midst of as great a revival of religion as New Haven ever witnessed. Realizing the position of the young man, and fearing that he would be crushed and the cause he advocated be injured, I deemed it a privilege as well as a duty to "throw a rope," and, if possible, save him from the wicked persecutions surrounding him. I do not propose to go into a full narrative of this wicked combination, but I cannot in justice to the cause of Christ and my personal friends, say other than this: the young preacher was assailed to that extent by the professed followers of Christ as to partially give way for a time. In my family he found an asylum from those who would glory in driving him to abandon his religion and his Master's work. He was but two years old in the cause, his former life not in sympathy with the new, friends expecting that he could stand erect without extending their sympathy to sustain him. Instead of kindly Christian greeting, he was discarded. This was more than he could bear, and like John B. Gough, he fell (but only once), and had not that great man's friends thrown "the rope" four times, Mr. Gough would have fallen short the laurels he now carries in his gray hairs. Before high heaven myself and family had no axe to grind,

when we, like the Shunamite woman, introduced Marvin
W. Lutz into our plain " upper chamber." Our cruse of
oil was then full, but we remembered the warning,
" Touch not mine anointed, and do my prophets no
harm !"

The author has learned that Friendship, if available
when wanted, is Christianity. Forgive thine enemy
" seventy times seven." And now, to close this subject
and the book, let me say, with all solemnity and joy, I
believe that when Christ comes many " professors " (if
they finally enter his kingdom) will be surprised to see
Marvin W. Lutz there, but it will not surprise the
author. Amen! Amen!!